TRINITY RISING

By

J.E. Taylor

Trinity Rising © 2024 J.E. Taylor

TRINITY RISING

**Plans for a bright future disintegrate when
Lucifer comes to claim Damian and Naomi's
trinity child.**

Mornings are a challenge, with Damian being mortal. He instinctively dives for the floor when dawn's light illuminates the bed. The scald of whiskey, and the way Naomi feels, are the only constants which haven't changed. However, his mortal world shines when fatherhood hits his horizon.

Plans for a bright future disintegrate when Lucifer comes to claim their Trinity child, playing dirty by framing Damian for murder. Now, Damian and Naomi are on the run from both Lucifer and the law. They find an ally in a most unlikely source, ex-FBI agent Steve Williams and his family; a family with enough psychic energy to wage a war and realign the universe.

With their new friends as part of the dynamic, Damian and Naomi are desperate for victory against the devil. One wrong step and they could trigger Armageddon, or worse, the hope for our future could fall into Lucifer's greedy grip.

Trinity Rising
Chapter One
Damian

SUNSHINE.

I rolled onto the floor with my heart in my throat and panic gripping my muscles. It wasn't until I was on my hands and knees that I realized I had done it again. Naomi's chuckle from the bed immediately set the irritation switch in my head, and I glared over the edge of the mattress at her amused smile.

"That's never going to get old," she said and rolled on her side, propping her cheek in her palm.

I could have said something crude, but the humor in her eyes soothed the nasty comments right out of my vocabulary. Being human sucked much more than I remembered. The only thing that remained the same was the burn of a shot of whiskey and the way Naomi felt when we made love.

Everything else was a constant challenge, including taming my conditioned response to sunlight. You'd think after a little over a month, I wouldn't be throwing myself for cover when the sun hit the bed, but apparently, twenty-five-hundred years of fearing the fiery orb really did a job on my head.

"I'm glad I could amuse you," I said, opting to slip under the covers again for just a little longer before I had to crack open my computer to work on a few coding jobs thrown my way. Now that I was mortal, I didn't need to save like I had in the past. Because of my frugal nature, I had amassed more money than we could ever hope to spend in one lifetime, but even with the ridiculous sum in my bank account, I couldn't just sit on my ass doing nothing.

Naomi started writing. I think it's a form of therapy for her, especially considering the hell she's been through since she met me. Her purging of dark things onto the pages of a book seemed to quiet the nightmares.

I reached for her, pushing a strand of her dark hair behind her ear before giving her a quick morning kiss. When I pulled away, the soft smile on her lips morphed into a grimace and her hand shot over her mouth. Before I knew what was happening, she was out of the bed and running for the bathroom.

Retching sounds came from the half-closed door and I slid out of bed, crossing the distance.

"Sick?" I asked, even though the answer was obvious.

She nodded, wiping her mouth with a tissue before flushing the bile away. I crossed and put my wrist to her forehead. Cool skin met mine.

"You don't feel like you've got a fever."

She climbed to her feet and stepped to the sink, brushing her teeth and spitting before she dignified my comment with an answer.

"My stomach has been queasy for a couple of days."

"Maybe Val can look at you," I offered and grabbed my toothbrush, washing my morning breath away.

"I'm feeling better now; maybe it was just something I ate."

I turned toward her, raising a brow. "Are you complaining about my cooking already?"

"No." Her light laugh filled the bathroom.

The music of her laugh set me in motion and I caught her by the waist, pulling her close.

"You don't want to catch this," she said, arching away from me.

"I don't really care." I kept my grip on her waist, holding her against me and letting my hands wander to the edge of the baby-doll nightgown. She wiggled in my grasp and all I could do was smile at the color filling her cheeks.

"Come on," she whispered, but this time she was less resistant and trying to suppress a smile.

I dipped my mouth to the side of her neck, nibbling my way from her ear to her shoulder. "Are you sure I can't interest you in a nice, long, hot shower?" I asked and worked my way back up the same line to her earlobe. She didn't object, and her sigh of concurrence brought a grin to my lips. I knew I probably should let her go back to bed and rest, but my appetite for her had grown since my transition from immortal to human and I couldn't seem to get enough.

What little clothing we had fell onto the floor and I navigated her into the shower. The water seemed to rejuvenate Naomi, and she was the one to push me against the wall, covering my mouth with the kind of kiss that made me want to sink to my knees in worship.

She knew how to make me forget everything with a touch—forgetting millennia and all that came before her. She erased it all and I could only fathom the moment. Making love to her was a slice of heaven, a dance of rhythms and movement in such unity that I swear this is what fate had planned for me all along.

Music blasted in the living room, and I chuckled against Naomi's neck.

"I think we disrupted Valerie's studies again," I whispered and kissed her exposed throat.

Naomi purred in that erotic way that made my skin tingle and I pulled away, studying her flushed features and the dripping mane of hair, running my hands through the silky strands before covering her mouth in an all-consuming kiss.

Trinity Rising
Chapter Two
Damian

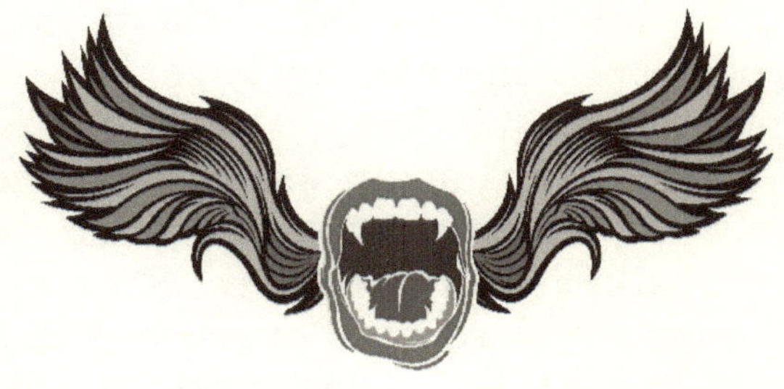

NAOMI STEPPED INTO MY office holding something plastic in her hand. The way she bit her lip as she stared at the thing pulled my full attention. I hated that worried look; it plagued my mind and brought up unpleasant memories of life on the run.

"What?"

She turned the front of what she held towards me and I stared at the little plus in the middle of the plastic before bringing my gaze to hers. I had seen enough commercials over the years to have an idea of what I was looking at, but I wasn't prepared for the onslaught of emotion that little plus sign sent parading through my bloodstream.

"Is that what I think it is?"

She nodded, and joy burst from the center of my being. I had no memory of crossing the distance, but when I came back to reality, I had her in my arms, twirling in a circle, and my smile actually made my cheeks ache.

"Are you sure?" I asked, setting her down.

"Yes. Valerie made me do the test twice."

Naomi was more subdued than I would have expected and I put my enthusiasm in check, lifting her chin so she met my gaze.

"Aren't you excited?"

She bit her lip again, and I dialed it in completely as a new worry bit under my skin. We'd never talked about children. Ever.

Even after we were both cured of the shadow virus, so maybe my assumptions that she wanted the same thing I did was flawed.

"Did you... want children?" I asked. I tried to keep the strained hesitation out of my voice, but I didn't do a very good job.

The tension in her body loosened. "Yes, I want to have children with you, it's just..." she trailed off, and the conflict danced over her features, twitching her eyelids as she tried to articulate all that was going on under the surface.

"You're afraid," I finished, understanding her fears. Hell, I had them too, but mine were more about what sort of child we would produce as opposed to what Lucifer would do when he found out.

Her nod confirmed my statement. "If he ever got his hands on my child..." Naomi couldn't finish, and she pulled me into a fierce hug. "I don't know what I'd do."

I wrapped my arms around her and kissed her temple. "I have a feeling that'll be the least of our worries."

She glanced up. The seriousness in her steady gaze told me she didn't quite understand my point.

"I'm not sure what's involved in raising a trinity," I said. "Especially if our child has some of the same... gifts that you have." For a moment, I envisioned being cornered by an angry tiger cub and couldn't help grinning.

"What's with that look?"

"What if the baby can change forms at will?" I opted to ask the question as opposed to sharing my little imagery.

Naomi sighed. "What if she can't?"

"She?"

Her lips pressed together, and I refocused on what she asked.

"Well, then *she* would be normal."

Her eyes rolled, and she laughed for the first time since she gave me the news. "You really think we're capable of having a normal child?"

I answered with an almost imperceptible lift of my shoulders, along with a grin. "As long as the child is healthy, who the hell cares if she's normal or not?"

Her cheeks dimpled and laugh lines appeared at the corner of her eyes. Any worry that had been there a few minutes ago seemed to evaporate in her budding glow.

"Have I told you I loved you lately?"

She beamed and nodded, pulling me into another hug. "I love you, too," she said and unwrapped her arms. Naomi literally bounced out of the room and I imagined she continued that flighty step all the way to the family room upstairs.

I stared after her, and my smile slowly faded. She had every right to be afraid and so did I. If Lucifer got wind of this, regardless of whatever condition he was in, he'd crawl out of hell to stop it. God only knows what would happen then.

I closed my eyes, and my chin dropped to my chest. I've never been a praying man, but right now, we needed all the protection the angels in heaven could provide.

"Michael, she's pregnant," I whispered, knowing damn well he couldn't hear me from within our sanctuary. Just saying it aloud sent a jolt of excitement along with a profound stab of fear through my body, tingling through my cells and producing a rash of gooseflesh.

I shivered and saved my work, shutting down my computer before putting on an appropriate smile and heading upstairs into the loud music and laughter.

AFTER DINNER, NAOMI BEGGED off early, looking every bit as tired as she said she was. I gave her a goodnight peck and settled into the couch with the remote. I must have clicked through the channels twice before Valerie cleared her throat. I glanced in her direction.

"Feel like a game of chess?" Valerie asked, closing her medical books.

"Sure." I hadn't played a game with her since we came back from Colorado and now that both Naomi and I were back in what Valerie dubbed healthy-land, I figured I could go without a night of aimless television and I turned it off.

She retrieved the beautifully carved chess set I had given her for her birthday and sat down on the couch next to me. I took the black marble pieces and set them up opposite her light set. I caught her glancing toward the hallway and cocked my head, sending her a silent question. She shook her head and tapped her watch.

"What's up?"

"Not yet," she whispered and picked up the remote for the stereo, turning it on low.

"Okay," I said and nodded toward the board. "It's your move."

She smirked and dropped her gaze to the board. For the first time since we got back, I took a moment to study her. The resemblance to Michael came through in the thick, wavy hair and the perfectly proportioned facial features, both qualities that also resonated in my wife, but unlike Naomi, Valerie didn't have a hint of Native American in her complexion or raven-black hair.

She made her first move and leaned back into the cushions, meeting my gaze.

"Are you checking me out?"

I chuckled and glanced at the chessboard. "I never noticed just how much you look like Naomi," I said and countered her move without much thought.

A dimple appeared in her cheek and she pressed her lips into a tight smile.

I crossed my arms and leaned back, challenging her to say what was behind that look. When she said nothing, I smiled. "Wasn't it a couple of months ago that you were checking me out?"

"So you were checking me out." Her arms tightened across her chest, closing me off with non-verbal cues.

"No, I was studying you a little closer, noticing similarities and differences between you and Naomi. At least I was looking at your face and not your ass." I had to add that last point, especially after her not-so-subtle check of my backside when we first came here.

A rose hue bloomed in each of her cheeks and she looked away. Instead of dignifying me with an answer, she concentrated on the chessboard. After a few moments, a knight moved, and she glanced at me expectantly.

"What did you want to talk to me about?" I said, lowering my voice to barely a whisper before focusing on the game in front of me. I sat staring at the chessboard, contemplating my next move, when Valerie cleared her throat. Reaching out, I moved one of my rooks and then focused back on her.

"I ran a couple of tests," she said, shifting on the seat like she suddenly couldn't find a comfortable position.

"Naomi said you made her do a couple of pregnancy tests."

When she met my gaze and tilted her head in that puppy dog way, it made my blood freeze in my veins. Valerie wasn't talking about the pregnancy tests.

"What?" I hissed.

"Besides coming back as undoubtedly pregnant, the results showed a very high level of glucose."

I shrugged. I had no idea what that meant, but based on the concern written in the crease between her eyes, I knew it couldn't be good.

"I need her to get tested for diabetes."

The answer didn't strike the kinds of alarms it would have if the word had been cancer or something equally as deadly.

"Okay," I said, stretching the word out.

"Damian, diabetes could kill both her and the child if left unchecked."

She now had my full attention, and an icy dread blanketed me. I tried to swallow, but my mouth had gone dry. Instead of speaking, I nodded for her to go on.

"Whether it's gestational diabetes, or regular diabetes, there could be complications with the pregnancy. Serious complications."

I blinked. "You are telling me Naomi could die?"

"Yes, if she has diabetes, there is a much higher chance of... issues."

"Issues?"

"Short term, long term, there's a wide range of problems that can occur for both her and the baby," she said.

The lack of full disclosure grated on my nerves. "Tell me the range," I demanded, leaning my elbows on my knees and just staring at the floor as she went from the least severe consequences of having to watch her diet for the rest of her life, to the most catastrophic, which made my eyelids draw closed and my head dip against the pressure.

I swallowed and tried to ask the question twice before my voice would pass over the sudden block in my throat. "Are you telling me we might have to make a choice between her and the baby?"

She remained quiet, meeting my gaze with neither a nod nor a shake of her head. "I don't know. Let's get her properly tested first before you start turning over the different doomsday scenarios in your head. It could also just be a side effect of her DNA makeup. The ability to still change into a tiger could screw with the tests."

Irritation snaked into my blood and I stood, crossing to the sliders, choosing to stare out at the backyard instead of snapping at Valerie. She was just trying to keep me informed, but I would have much preferred being in the dark on this one.

I knew without a doubt Naomi would choose the baby, and I glanced at the stars spattering the early spring sky, wondering just how many times we could face death before it claimed us.

"It's your turn," Valerie said after a few minutes.

"I know." I didn't return to the game yet, contemplating moves between the chessboard and my life. With a sigh, I walked back and moved my king, giving Valerie a half-hearted shrug before leaving her with my sacrifice.

THE ASTON-MARTIN STILL wasn't running as smoothly as I wanted, especially after the joy ride Naomi took it on when she saved my ass from Lucifer; I always ended up in the garage when something was eating at me. It was better than tossing and turning in bed and disrupting Naomi's sleep.

Valerie didn't bother following me into the basement, and I'm glad. I needed time to figure out exactly what options I had. The more I fiddled under the hood, the more I realized it was as much of a crapshoot as stepping off our property into the unprotected world.

The one thing mortality gave me was perspective.

My time was finite now, and I wanted a long, happy life with Naomi, and a hoard of children. The light flickered above me and I glanced up from the underside of the hood, catching the sway of the single bulb.

I leaned to the side and caught her blank stare.

"What are you doing?" Naomi asked, rubbing her sleepy eyes.

"Tinkering." I grabbed the hand cloth and wiped the grease off my fingers, stepping around the engine into full view.

"Why?"

"Couldn't sleep," I answered and tossed the rag onto the side of the engine block.

Worry bloomed in her eyes and I crossed the distance between us. I stopped and stared down into her upturned face, wondering how in the world I would survive without her. Instead of voicing my concerns, I leaned down, pressing my lips to hers in a soft kiss.

"What are you doing up at this hour?" I asked, changing the subject.

"I had a nightmare." She wrapped her arms around her waist and shivered. "It seemed so real and when I woke up, you weren't there."

I knew what that was like. Our nightmares were a blend of the near-death experiences and Lucifer's promises. She sometimes woke screaming, trying to unwrap from the blanket like they were the beasts assaulting her. Those were the ones that made my blood boil. Even though Lucifer never made good on his promise to make her his whore, it still played havoc with both our minds. The rest of them involved seeing each other die in various excruciating ways. I didn't know which flavor she had tonight, and I really didn't want to know. Not after the real-world news I'd been turning over in my head for the last couple of hours.

"Sorry, babe," I said and lead her back to the stairwell leading to the underground tunnel. I grabbed the flashlight before flipping the switch off on the overhead bulb. Drenched in darkness, I reached for her, finding her hand before flipping the flashlight on.

She didn't speak as I led her back to the bedroom in the main house and I didn't press her for details. We both still had nightmares, and only the word was necessary.

"You died," she said when we reached our room and I closed the door.

Naomi couldn't shake that nightmare. She described it once, saying her blood left me like it had the other vampire and she crumbled, unable to fight Lucifer. It always ended with her scream of terror as he came for her.

I ran my palm over her cheek and pulled her to my chest. My nightmares didn't end with her dying. In mine, I lived long enough for the sun to burn and Lucifer to ravage her before I turned to dust.

"It wasn't the usual."

Her tone surprised me, and I searched the shadows of her gaze, looking for insight, but found none. I lifted my eyebrows, waiting for her to enlighten me.

She shook her head. "Just go clean up and come to bed."

Who was I to argue?

After washing my hands and brushing my teeth, I stripped down to my boxers and climbed into the bed. Her back was to me and I curved around her, pulling her to my chest and planting a kiss on her shoulder.

"Are you all right?" I asked when silence blanketed the room.

I thought she had fallen asleep, but she shifted and sighed.

"I'm not sure."

I waited, knowing if I pushed her, she'd just clam up until she was ready. Finally, when she didn't continue, I propped myself up on my elbow and leaned over her, getting a glimpse of her face in the splintered moonlight. The glistening paths on her cheeks gave me a start.

"Are you crying?"

Naomi met my gaze and the gloss filling her eyes confirmed my question and tugged at my heart.

"Babe, it was only a nightmare."

In a flash, her arms encircled my neck, and she pulled me down into her grasp.

"I lost everything," she whispered.

I held her tight, whispering, "shhh." until the quakes rocking her form settled.

"Naomi," I said when she stopped shaking. She peeled away and stared into my eyes. "I'm not planning on dying for a long time," I added when I had her full attention.

"Sometimes planning and reality don't meet," she said and sniffled.

"Neither one of us is clairvoyant," I pointed out.

She wiped her eyes and nodded. "I know, it's just... it was disturbing."

Her trembling lips propelled me forward, and I covered them with mine, tasting the soft saltiness of tears mingling with her natural sweetness, and I sighed, breaking the kiss. She palmed my cheek and attempted to smile. It didn't work quite as well as she might have thought, but I let it go. I really didn't want to hear about whatever nightmarish horror she could dream up.

Instead, I snuggled down into my pillow, pulled her back into the spoon position, and ran my fingers slowly through her hair. It wasn't long before she dropped into dreamland and her chest started the soft rise and fall of sleep.

Trinity Rising
Chapter Three
Damian

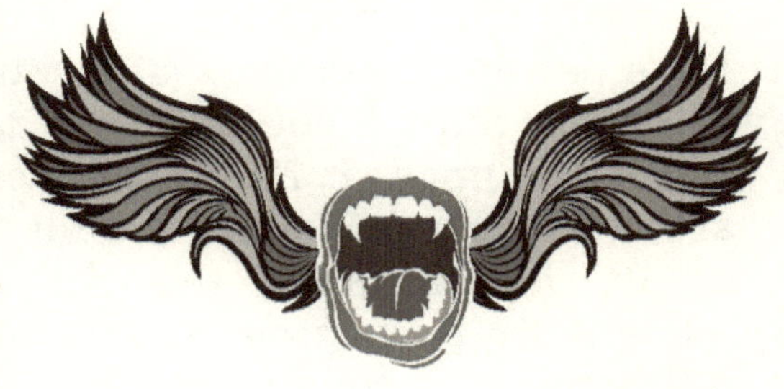

I WOKE FACING AWAY from the window and my gaze landed on the sunlight painting the walls with the outline of the windowpanes standing out like a giant Braille relief map. Instead of the usual freak out, I sighed and studied the patterns that so many take for granted.

The door to the bathroom opened, and I rolled onto my back, looking down beyond the foot of the bed at Naomi. Her hair glistened in the morning sun and the soft smile on her lips created a heat through my entire form. I sat up, returning her smile.

"Valerie is taking me to the doctor. Did you want to come?"

My smile faded. Neither of us had left the safety of the property since the battle with Lucifer and just the thought left me chilled. All the *what-ifs* hit, and I stared at her. Instead of voicing the shit flinging in my head, I gave her a nod and threw the blankets aside. Any hope I had of morning sex went out the window and I headed for the bathroom, catching a quick kiss on my way by.

If she was nervous about leaving, I couldn't tell, but that's par for the course. She could hide her nerves better than I could. Yesterday was one of the first times I had ever seen her hesitant about anything. Naomi usually barrels along without much of a thought to her mortality. It's both refreshing and frustrating, and one of the many reasons I loved her.

The warm water of the shower didn't quell the chill in my bones either, and I wondered if we could get someone to come here instead of venturing out. Sure, I had gone to the garage, but that place was almost as secure as this one. The only saving grace was it was bright and sunny, so the monsters that hunted at night wouldn't be on the prowl.

That left demons.

I hated demons. Those crazy fucks didn't have any sort of moral code. They plundered, tortured, and killed with glee.

By the time I stepped into the living room, I had worked myself up into a foul mood.

"What time is your appointment?" I asked with a clip in my voice that turned both women's heads.

"What crawled up your ass?" Valerie shot back.

I leveled a glare in her direction. "We haven't left the house since..." I stopped, pressing my lips together and shifting my stance. I knew

Valerie's motives were purely to make sure Naomi was okay, but I don't think she considered what could happen on the outside.

"I've been coming to and from without incident."

She had a point. Even with Uncle Ted off on vacation, no one bothered her. I nodded and met Naomi's gaze. "What if demons are watching the place? We have to be prepared for the worst."

That annoyed crease appeared between her eyes and her arms crossed. She didn't need to speak to broadcast her irritation, but underneath the fire burning in her gaze, I saw the first hint of hesitation.

"How does one prepare for a demon attack?" she asked, opting for the snarky sarcasm that always steeled my nerves.

I shrugged. "I used to be able to smell them coming." My hands found their way into my pockets and I dropped my gaze.

"You don't have to come if you don't want to."

My gaze snapped to hers and I bit back my comment. There was no way in hell I was going to let her go without me. I turned to Valerie.

"Do you have your uncle's pistol?"

"You don't have a permit to conceal and carry. Besides, the hospital frowns upon firearms on the premise unless you're a police officer," she said.

I just stared at her because anything that came out of my mouth would have turned into a rant. Instead, I just nodded and clenched my jaw. "Fine," I uttered after her challenging stare down.

Valerie crossed into the kitchen and opened a drawer. It slammed closed, and she stepped back into my line of sight, tossing something in my direction. I caught the small pouch and stared at the pot-pourri wrapped in sheer webbing. "There's already one in her pocketbook. Put it in your coat pocket and whatever badass is in the neighborhood leaves you alone."

"What the hell is this?" I snapped.

"It masks the scent of our bloodline."

"How?" I asked, this time with more patience, bringing the bag up to my nose to take a whiff. I pulled it away fast, but the sickly sweet stench hung on the air, making my eyes water.

"Michael gave them to me."

"He had a way to... hide you from..." I trailed off, looking at the small package again. The scent was repulsive, yet familiar. I blinked, and the origin of that smell slammed into my brain, making my gaze snap back to Valerie. "With demon blood?"

Both Naomi and Valerie blanched at the revelation. Naomi even moved her purse farther away from her body in an unconscious reflex of disgust.

"It works," Valerie said.

I didn't want the thing to touch me and I put it in the side pocket of my jacket, zipping it almost the entire way closed. Wiping my hands on my jeans, I gave a nod. "So, what time is her appointment?" I asked again, but this time without the edge.

VALERIE DROVE WITH NAOMI and me crammed in the small back seat of the truck.

The tiny side windows were tinted, and the back had a stencil of the American Flag blocking the window, so we were virtually invisible to the outside traffic. I still tensed when we got into a more populated area.

The half glances toward the truck had more to do with the rumbling engine than the occupants, and by the time we drove into the medical center in Torrington, I had relaxed enough to let my guard down. The moment the truck shut off, the nerves jumped into action.

Valerie stepped out of the truck and pushed the seat down for us to exit. I got out and my gaze bounced around the quiet parking lot before I turned and helped Naomi out of the cab. I felt like a secret service agent protecting the President in a crowd. My gaze couldn't move fast enough over the blacktop and cars looking for threats. By the time we got to the door, I was wrapped so tight I almost attacked an old woman who pushed open the doors on her way out of the office building.

Valerie and Naomi gave me that shocked expression that I was used to, and I let out a small laugh. I knew my strength and speed were superior to most humans, but if we encountered a demon, I would only be as effective as a fly swatter.

In the waiting room, I sat next to Naomi and my leg bounced in nervous anticipation. My back was safe against a wall, but the office had a half dozen other women in attendance and just the proximity to anything remotely dangerous left me on edge.

Naomi placed her hand on my knee, and I turned, meeting her gaze.

"Everything will be okay," she whispered, pushing down until my leg stopped moving.

I covered her hand with mine and gave it a squeeze, exhaling and offering a tight smile. It was a long half hour wait.

"Anna Andreas?" the nurse asked.

Naomi didn't respond at first, but I gave her hand a squeeze and nodded toward the nurse.

"Oh," she mumbled and collected her purse. She gave Valerie a quick glance and stood. I followed suit, and the nurse gave me that high browed what do you think you're doing glare.

"It's okay if my husband comes in with me, right?" Naomi asked when she caught the nurse's less than subtle glare.

The nurse dropped her gaze to Naomi's, and it softened. She nodded, but when it drifted back in my direction, the hard lines filled in around her mouth. When Naomi disappeared into the bathroom, I started nibbling on my nail, waiting for her to return. The nurse waited patiently, but ignored me long enough for my nerve endings to tingle.

"I guess you see a lot of nervous husbands," I finally said to break the ice, but the look she sent my way chilled me further. There would be no ice breaking with this one. I peeled off my coat and hung it on the chair, crossing to the window. I did a quick scan of the asphalt view.

"How old are you anyway?" the nurse asked, and I glanced over my shoulder.

When she asked my age, I caught my smirk in the glass's reflection and wondered how she'd react if I told her my actual age. Instead, I turned, meeting her gaze. "I'm twenty-five."

"Pft. You shouldn't be thinking about a family yet. Get established first," she scoffed at me, but at least the hostility was waning.

I glanced at my coat. Maybe it was the sachet that made her act like the ice princess, and the minute I took my jacket off and put some distance between me and my coat, she thawed. "We're good," I said and crossed my arms, leaning on the windowsill and waiting for Naomi.

"Do you realize just how much raising a child costs?" she chided.

"Yes, ma'am, I'm aware," I said. "I'm also aware of what the projections for college are," I added for good measure, punctuating it with a smile.

Her frown eased, and she gave me a nod just as the door opened and Naomi stepped inside, handing her a cup of urine.

"The doctor will be with you in a moment," the nurse said and stepped out with the offering.

Naomi took a seat, and I stepped to her side, taking her hand in mine.

"I think those things Valerie gave us make normal people hostile," I whispered. "Either that, or the nurse needs lessons in bedside manners."

Naomi giggled and squeezed my hand. "Or she's just reacting to your projected paranoia."

The shock of her words went through me like a sound wave vibrating up my spine and into my teeth. I raised my brow. "It's that obvious?"

"Um...yeah," she answered. Her lips twitched into a smile. "It would be highly amusing if I wasn't just as nervous as you are."

"I think once the baby is born, we should start looking for somewhere else to live," I said.

Her smile faded.

Before she could answer, the door opened and a tall, bespectacled man wearing a white lab coat stepped into the room. He looked from the laptop in his hands to Naomi and me, breaking into a broad grin.

"I guess you two are expecting," he said and placed the computer on the counter before offering Naomi his hand. "I'm Dr. Wolk."

"Na... Anna," Naomi said, catching herself before she revealed her real name. "And this is my husband, Damian."

Dr. Wolk extended his hand to me, and I shook it, meeting his open gaze. His grip was firm, but not overbearing.

"Congratulations," he said and adjusted his glasses before bringing his gaze back to Naomi. "When was your last period?"

Naomi bit her lip and glanced at me. She couldn't very well say five years ago and I'm not sure she had one between being shot with the cure and when I woke from my coma. I just shrugged. She hadn't had one since I came out of it.

"Do you have a calendar?" she asked.

The doctor pointed to the wall behind her.

Naomi hopped off the table and ran her fingers over the dates, silently moving her mouth in thought. She tapped the date that she woke from her delirium in Colorado and ran her finger over the calendar from that point, hesitating over the day we almost died.

A couple of weeks out from that, she tapped the date.

"February third," she said.

I woke up a week later.

"And I'm pretty sure we conceived on the tenth or soon thereafter."

The tenth was that first day in the shower, and the memory stirred my soul. I had mustered up enough energy to make love to her in the shower and then all strength left me. She dried me off and helped me pull on a clean pair of shorts while I sat on the bathroom floor, dizzy and exhausted. Naomi had to enlist Valerie's help to get me back to the bedroom. I remember feeling helpless as they changed the bed, and once I was tucked into the clean sheets, Valerie hooked me back up to the IV. It took me a few days of eating and sleeping to get up the energy to make love to her again, but after those celibate days in the beginning, we haven't missed a daily romp.

She smiled at me and climbed back on the table.

The doctor nodded and typed the information on the computer. "Well, based on that, it looks like you're due around October 20th." He scanned the screen, and a frown formed before he moved his gaze to Naomi.

"I'd like you to have some blood drawn and do a couple of tests before you leave today to make sure we have your glucose levels under control."

"What's wrong with my glucose level?" Naomi asked.

"It's high enough to pass into your urine, which isn't necessarily cause for alarm, but I'd just like to make sure we aren't looking at a potential complication. Did you have anything to eat this morning?"

Naomi shook her head and the flash of concern in Dr. Wolk's eyes before he moved his gaze to the numbers on the screen lit my stomach on fire.

"Is there a history of diabetes in your family?" he asked, scanning the information from the sheet she filled out in the waiting room.

"Not to my knowledge."

She reached out and took my hand in a grip that I had encountered before. The one that announced her nerves jumping into overtime.

The doctor glanced up at her and offered a smile. "I'll send Leticia back in to take some blood," he said and stood. "It will take a few minutes to run the tests and then I'll be back in and see if we can detect a heartbeat, okay?"

We both nodded and the moment the door closed, she turned her dark gaze in my direction. The worry there made me swallow and try on a smile.

"Everything will be just fine," I said, and the conviction in my voice surprised me. Based on the conversation with Valerie, I had my doubts, but it was something under our control and it was my turn to be strong.

I leaned forward and planted a kiss on her forehead, smoothing her hair back with my free hand. She closed her eyes and leaned her cheek on my palm in that endearing way that squeezed my heart.

The door opened, and a different nurse stepped inside. The way she glanced into the hallway and shut the door prickled my nerves. When she turned full toward us, I knew we were in trouble.

"Where's the other nurse?" Naomi asked, her eyes dropping to the tray the nurse set on the counter. The needle and glass vials were expected, but the glistening scalpel was not.

Her red-eyed glare snapped to both of us and she reached for the knife, but I was faster. I slapped my hand down on the corner of the tray, sending everything across the room with a loud clatter. The only thing between this demon and Naomi was me. And she stepped forward, her face transforming into an angry growl.

"What do you think you're doing?" she snarled.

A sound behind her drew her attention and her expression transitioned to embarrassment for the benefit of the head nurse now standing in the open door.

"I was just about to ask you the same question." The head nurse glanced beyond her subordinate without any of the attitude she had given me earlier. Instead, her underling looked down at the mess on the floor and back in her direction.

"Isn't this the room for the D-and-C?"

"We don't have a D-and-C patient today, Clara," the nurse said. There was a clear warning in her tone and her icy glare landed on the younger nurse. "This isn't the first time you've made that mistake." She crossed her arms.

Clara sent visual daggers in my direction before glancing back at her superior.

"Please leave," the head nurse said in a tone that left no negotiation.

"But, Leticia," Clara started, but Nurse Leticia pointed toward the exit.

"Now."

I stepped closer to Naomi, still buffering her from the inept demon and, for a moment, I thought the bitch was going to lash out at Leticia. Her fists clenched, and she shot a glare in my direction before stomping out of the office.

Leticia sighed and stepped inside. "I'm sorry about that. Clara is new, and she's been a disaster since she started." She squatted to pick up the syringe and the vials and hesitated when her gaze fell on the scalpel. A dark shadow crossed her features, and she shook her head, picking up the instrument with her thumb and forefinger, like it carried a nasty disease.

She sat back on her haunches, and the crease between her eyes grew. She glanced up at me before standing. I still blocked Naomi, but when the offending knife and needle dropped into the sharps container, I stepped aside.

"I'll need to get a clean syringe and vials," she said and slipped out of the room, leaving the door open.

I glanced at Naomi.

"What the hell was that?" she whispered.

"A demon," I answered, and the remaining splotches of color in her cheeks faded.

Naomi's hand slid over her abdomen in a protective gesture and I stepped closer, reaching for her hand.

"How'd you know?"

I smiled and glanced over my shoulder at the door before answering. "I've been around a lot longer than you, hun."

She nodded, and her gaze moved behind me.

"Okay, let's see if I can get some blood for those tests the doctor ordered," Leticia said, and I yielded, letting her approach Naomi. She gave me a nod of approval and I locked my gaze with my wife's.

"Are you okay?" I asked. She still hadn't regained any color, and when she shrugged, I followed her gaze to the needle. Reaching out, I turned her chin toward me so she didn't have to watch the drawing of blood. It didn't bother me in the slightest, hell it actually made my stomach growl. I offered her a smirk when she tilted her head in a silent question.

The nurse finished and left the room.

"Are you serious?"

I laughed and gave her a shrug of my own. "What'd you expect?" I asked. "I'm still freaked by sunshine, so it's not odd that the sight of blood still makes me hungry. Twenty-five-hundred years of conditioning."

"You are too funny sometimes," she whispered and pulled me to her lips.

I didn't want to dampen her light mood with what I expected waited for us outside, but I also didn't want Valerie to be hit in the crossfire. After Naomi pulled away, I crossed to my coat and dug my phone out of the inside pocket. I typed a quick text that I was sure would draw a tremor of fear through Valerie, but she had the sachet on her, so the demons might not take notice of her.

"Valerie?" Naomi asked when I turned and dropped the phone in my shirt pocket.

"Yes. I told her to meet us out back. We aren't going in the way we came."

The door opened, interrupting our conversation, and I turned to see Dr. Wolk stepping into the room with what looked like a small stereo speaker. "The initial blood tests don't look as bad as I anticipated; however, we are sending a couple of the vials out for more tests just to make sure you are not at risk. I will want you to do the glucose screening at 24 weeks, but in the meantime, I'd like to take a listen." He slid into the chair next to the bed and lowered the back before pulling up Naomi's shirt to reveal her abdomen. He tucked a sheet in her pants, tugging them down so her entire belly showed.

I stared at her and for the first time; I saw the slight change in her stomach. It was no longer the flat washboard I was used to, and I wondered how I could have missed the nuance of change in her. Of course, I had been dealing with the strangeness of being human again after so long, but that still didn't excuse my lack of noticing the changes in her body.

The doctor ran a thin line of clear gel on Naomi's belly and pulled a thick wand from the side of the speaker. "I'm just warning you, it's extremely rare to hear the heartbeat at this early stage, so if we can't find it, I don't want you to worry."

"Okay," Naomi said.

I squeezed her hand as she tucked the pillow under her head and stared at the ceiling. A smile formed, and I glanced up. Taped above the table was one of those posters of Anne Geddes baby gardens.

Dr. Wolk glanced up and echoed both our smiles. "I try to give my patient's something unique. There's a different picture in each room," he said and the wand touched Naomi, running slowly across the path of gel.

The volume was turned to high and the noises echoing from the speaker sounded like an underwater wonderland. A slight fluttering sound came and went, and the doctor retraced his path, finding the flutter again. He looked up at Naomi with a grin.

"You are one lucky girl. Six weeks is usually early for a heartbeat, but there it is," he said and pulled the wand away from her belly, wiping the gel with a cloth and pulling her shirt down once she was clean. "I'll want to see you next week so we can go over the test results. You can set up your next appointment at the front desk before you leave." Dr. Wolk stood and gave a nod as he exited the room.

The reality that the woman I loved was carrying my child hit, and I bit down on my lip to push the swirl of emotions away. I smiled at her and brought her hand to my lips. Her eyes sparkled with unshed tears and she wrapped her arms around me, using my height to get to her feet.

"We're having a baby," she said and her voice cracked. She buried her face in my chest and the first wave of tears struck.

I blinked my eyes clear and kissed the top of her head. "I love you," I said when I was sure I had a handle on my voice. Since I met her, she was the more emotionally stable of the two of us. Now it was my turn to be strong.

After scheduling Naomi's next appointment, I checked my phone; there was nothing from Valerie, so I stuck my head into the waiting room. Her seat was empty and my gaze shot to the parking lot. The truck still sat where we parked it and icy dread filled my veins.

Instead of heading out of the office area, I turned toward the desk.

"We have a bit of a drive. Is there a restroom my wife could use before we get on the road?"

Naomi's lips pressed into an embarrassed smile. The girl pointed toward the way we had come.

"Down the hall and around the corner on your right."

I took Naomi's hand and led her farther into the office, looking for one specific thing; when we turned the corner, my nerves relaxed a fraction. Before we could be intercepted, I pulled her through the exit, into a small stairwell and put my hand over her mouth, shaking my head before closing the door as quietly as I could.

I glanced between her and the stairs leading down to a lower entrance before maneuvering her into the darkest corner. I pulled my phone out without speaking and typed a text to Valerie, telling her they were running another test, so we would be another fifteen minutes.

I put my finger on my lips and showed Naomi the text before making sure my phone was on silent. She didn't understand until I hit send and Valerie's ringtone echoed through the stairwell.

"Fuck," an unfamiliar voice muttered from below, and Naomi's eyes widened.

I glanced at the stairs leading up and pulled her with me, silently climbing to the next floor. The door didn't have a handle, so we continued to the third floor.

This one had a knob, and I closed my eyes, saying a small prayer, and turned. It gave, and I opened it to another hall, moving Naomi into the carpeted stretch before shutting the door.

"What is going on?"

"Demons have Valerie," I whispered and continued down toward the other end of the hall. I wanted Naomi out of the building before they figured out our game, but I had no idea how I was going to get Valerie away from the bastards. I stopped at the next exit and leaned against the door, running my hand down my face before meeting Naomi's gaze.

"I wish she had let me take the gun," I said, pushing the fear down into my already knotted stomach.

"What are we going to do?" she asked and her hand went into that protective reflex, covering her abdomen without knowledge of the move.

"We aren't going to do anything. You are going to stay here and I'm going to take care of those bastards." I recognized the shadow that traveled over her features before they hardened into that stubborn aggravation I was used to. I shook my head before she opened her mouth to argue. "No. You're carrying my child. You aren't going out there until I know it is safe."

Naomi's lips thinned and she turned her back on me, crossing her arms and surveying the hall. She glanced over her shoulder, sending a glare at me before she marched away. Halfway down the hall sat a fire alarm box and when she reached for it, I almost laughed. Leave it to my wife to find a valid way out that wouldn't leave us alone in the parking lot with the enemy.

She pulled down and as the alarms broke out, wailing throughout the building, she passed in front of me and pushed open the door leading to a set of stairs on the opposite side of the floor. We joined a group of people clearing the building in an orderly fashion.

We exited at the far side of the parking lot, and I didn't want to leave Naomi alone in the crowd. At least one demon knew what she looked like and if I left her alone, I'm sure that's when all hell would break loose.

"Follow me," I whispered and navigated the parking lot, which was easier than I thought, especially with all eyes on the building, including the demon bitch that sat in the passenger seat.

Valerie sat still, her gaze locked in front of her, unfocused, even as we passed her line of sight. Her waxy skin glistened with sweat and I wondered what the hell held her in place. When we were a car away, I pulled Naomi lower.

"Stay here."

She glanced at the truck and then back to me, her eyes pleading in that way that made me hesitate, but I put my hand up and turned, focusing on the truck. From our vantage point, we couldn't see the building, and I didn't know who else was working with the demon bitch of a nurse holding Valerie hostage.

I did a quick scan and then stepped to the side of the truck, yanking the passenger door open. The bitch's head snapped in my direction, but I reacted faster than she did. My fist connected, breaking her nose before she removed the knife buried in Valerie's side.

The anger that flared pulled a growl from my lips and I yanked the psycho nurse from the car, twisting her neck as I turned. The sickening crunch of bone bounced off the car and I dropped the limp body, turning toward Naomi.

"Hurry," I said and as soon as she was in the car, I closed the door and ran to the driver's side. Without thinking, I slid Valerie to the middle of the bench seat and turned the key hanging from the ignition.

The truck revved to life and I hit the gas, tearing through the parking lot as fast as I dared. The hospital emergency room wasn't far, and I chanced a glance at Valerie. The girl still stared out the window, almost like she was already...

I shook the thought out of my head. "Check her pulse," I ordered.

Naomi's shaking fingers reached into my peripheral vision, landing on Valerie's throat as I took the turn into the emergency room entrance.

"Does she have a pulse?" I barked and glanced around Valerie, meeting Naomi's frightened stare.

"I, I don't know," she said. I slammed the brakes, stopping the vehicle within a hair of the ambulance sitting in front of me, and jumped out.

"You can't park here," a heavy-set officer said as he stepped out of the sliding doors.

"My friend was stabbed," was all I said, yanking the passenger door open. Naomi hopped out and moved aside, so I could reach in for Valerie. I didn't hesitate; I scooped her up so the hilt of the blade faced the hospital. My heart dropped when she didn't react with even a grunt from the change in position. I marched past the cop without another look. Each step brought back a random memory of Valerie. Years of memories, of watching her grow, flooded my senses and I carried her right past the desk and into one of the exam rooms. I didn't have to speak. The blade and blood dripping a path from the car was all the hospital needed.

The emergency room staff descended like a pack of wild eagles, pushing us aside while they assessed the damage. Naomi pulled me back against the wall as they barked commands that didn't register. The sound of a heartbeat pulled me out of my stress-filled trance, yanking a breath of relief from my chest. The nursing staff herded us from the room, despite my protests.

"They are bringing her to surgery," someone said, and I glanced down at the owner of the voice. A petite nurse stood with her hand on my chest. The name tattooed on her shirt read Sara H - RN.

"Is she going to make it?" I asked, my voice unsteady. I cleared my throat, glancing at

Naomi, who stood next to me with the same shell-shocked stare I imagined I wore.

"Are you family?"

"She's my cousin," Naomi said, gaining the nurse's attention. "Is she going to be okay?"

"We have the best doctors working on her right now," she answered.

I closed my eyes, finding the wall with my hand.

"The waiting room is that way. I will come find you when I get word as to her condition. Okay?"

I nodded and threw my arm around Naomi, turning in the direction the nurse had pointed.

The officer waited by the door, swinging a set of keys from his finger. When I approached, the keys stilled, and he crossed to me.

"What happened, son?" he asked.

"I don't know," I said. "Valerie came into Dr. Wolk's office with us and she was in the waiting room last I knew. The fire alarm was pulled, and we went out to the truck and found her like that." I pointed a shaking finger toward the exam rooms.

"The police are processing your vehicle."

I glanced around him at the cop cars and crime scene tape and nodded. "I hope they find the son of a bitch..." I muttered and glanced back at the cop.

"Did you touch the knife?"

"No. I don't think either of us did." I glanced at Naomi.

"I didn't touch it. The only thing I did was feel for a pulse when you asked me to."

The cop seemed satisfied for the time being and pointed us to the waiting room. Another staff member approached and handed us a clipboard to fill out with Valerie's information. I stared at the blanks and then at Naomi. I had the name, address and date of birth down, but not much else, and I sighed, dropping my head into my hands.

"Michael," I whispered, calling on the power of heaven to perform yet another miracle.

Trinity Rising
Chapter Four
Damian

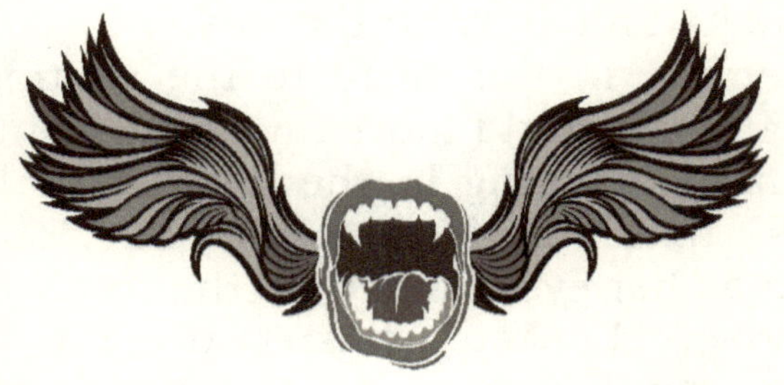

THE ONE GOOD THING about adrenaline is while it's running through your bloodstream; you're pretty much numb to emotions beyond the need to take action. When the battle ends and the adrenaline dries up, the wave crashes, and right now I was drowning in the thought of losing Valerie.

Naomi was doing her best to hold it together, but she barely contained her tears and the lack of response from our angelic relative was biting at my already raw nerves. I reached out, lacing my fingers through Naomi's, gave her my best reassuring smile, and brought the back of her hand to my lips.

Strength in the face of tragedy was not my most reliable trait, but I needed to put on the brave face for her. She sniffled and buried her face in my chest. I wrapped my arm around her and gave a squeeze, knowing damn well it wasn't enough to erase the soul-consuming fear.

I did not know who the other demon was, but I'd bet my fortune that they knew the outcome of Naomi's tests, which meant Lucifer would soon know we had a trinity on the way.

Movement in the entry to the waiting room caught my eye, and I moved my gaze from Naomi to the man standing in the doorway. I lowered Naomi's hand and straightened. Her gasp followed as her eyes landed on the same view.

"Michael?" I asked. I wasn't sure, not with the haggard being leaning on the doorframe. His slight nod kicked me into action and I dropped Naomi's grip, crossing the room and offering him a hand. He glanced at the offer and irritation raked over his face, but he took a hold of my arm and allowed me to lead him to the empty seat next to mine.

The young, vibrant angel I had known for all my days had finally aged... a lot. His once ebony hair was almost pure white and lines carved deep shadows in his face. Even his hands were wrinkled and gnarled. It took me a few minutes to find my voice.

"Can you... help?" I asked.

He gave my leg a pat. "I'm sorry." His chin dropped. "As you can see, I haven't had the chance to rejuvenate yet."

"What happened?" I couldn't help it, even though on some level I already knew.

He turned his gaze to mine. "I spent most of my energy on you, leaving just enough to make sure Naomi didn't bleed out." His gaze moved to Naomi, and he offered the slightest of smiles.

He had performed a miracle. I should have roasted in the sun, or at least dropped dead from the amount of blood loss and crushed bones in my body. But I hadn't because Michael swept in at the last minute and saved both of us. I just didn't realize what it had cost him.

I licked my lips and stared at the tile patterns traversing the floor.

"Will you ever..."

"Recuperate?" Michael finished my sentence and shrugged in a way that left my blood cold. "I honestly don't know."

"Valerie..." I started and fidgeted, picking at the hangnail on my thumb before I cleared my throat. "Valerie was stabbed."

"I know."

"By a demon," I added.

"I gathered it was something along those lines, especially since she asked for your protection," he said. "She wanted to make sure you two survived, even if she didn't."

"She..." Naomi started.

Michael put his hand up, stopping her from asking the question that swarmed my mind as well. "I have no more insight than that."

An angel without insight. Now I've heard it all, but I wasn't in the position to make a snide comment. Instead, I sighed and pinched the bridge of my nose.

Naomi's grip tightened on mine, and I turned. Something outside the window held her gaze. When I followed her gaze to the glass, my already chilled blood froze and my chest constricted like someone tied a complex and tight knot with my lungs.

Outside, the crazy nurse I killed stood next to Valerie's truck, staring at us through the window with a narrowed glare. She cracked her neck and smiled, and then her lips moved, reciting the unmistakable name that would bring the devil to our door.

Lucifer.

The freeze in my blood turned to the burn of adrenaline and I grabbed Michael's arm with my free hand, moving us with a speed I didn't think I still possessed. It wasn't vampire speed, but it was damn fast, especially while dragging an old man and my stunned wife.

I turned toward the belly of the hospital, looking for a way to escape our intertwined fates. My heart hammered in my temple, creating a beat my feet followed. The clap of thunder announced his arrival, but I didn't even chance a look. Instead, I found a staircase leading to the floor below.

It wasn't until I stood in the sparsely populated cafeteria that I stopped. Both Michael and Naomi huffed, their faces as red from exertion as I imagined mine, and I let them rest at the table near the door. Michael collapsed in the chair next to me, and Naomi took the one farthest away from the door.

Her head dropped to the table and the rise and fall of her back was enough for me to grab the nearest garbage can and slide it under her. She spit a couple of times and then nodded, and I moved the can back to the wall by the door. As I approached the table, the air in the cafeteria shifted and I stopped with my gaze locked on Naomi's.

I didn't need to turn to know Lucifer stood behind me, but I wondered if he was in the same condition as his brother. Michael stood and for a brief instance, I saw the fire flare in him, but it flickered and he grabbed the edge of the table to steady his feeble form.

I inhaled, and spun, facing the monster that was hell bent on destroying me. Lucifer stood before me in human form, but unlike Michael, he was still young. A bandage covered his neck and Eve's burning form had left more damage on the right side of the devil's face.

His gaze narrowed as he studied me, and then it transitioned to Michael.

"You fool. You gave him your grace?"

My skin flushed hot with those words. Michael's grace? Holy shit. The old angel stepped to my side, but I couldn't look at him. I was still processing Lucifer's words.

"Now all he needs is yours," Michael snarled, and Lucifer's clawed hand shot out, puncturing Michael's chest.

"He may have your grace, but I am claiming your soul."

Michael somehow produced a smile. "My soul belongs to God," he uttered.

Lucifer yanked, ripping the heart from Michael's body. A scream pierced the room and the shuffle of panicked footsteps filled the cafeteria. Michael collapsed on the floor and Lucifer stared at the heart, mesmerized as the muscle's contractions slowed until it was still.

I stared as well, unable to move, to allow my brain to grasp the death of my uncle or the words he uttered. It wasn't until Lucifer brought the heart to his lips that my paralysis broke and I stepped backwards, running into the table.

The beast ripped the heart in half, his eyes closing as he savored the taste, and I shivered with revulsion. My gaze darted around the now empty room and back to Lucifer. He swallowed the rest of Michael's heart and slowly licked his fingers.

"There's nothing quite like angel blood, even without the grace," he whispered. The burns on his face transformed before my eyes, healing and reforming to what he had been before the flaming vampire attacked him.

With blood dripping from his lips, he turned toward the cafeteria entry, where an officer stood with his gun drawn. The smile that formed set me in motion. Instead of attacking, I turned, grabbed Naomi, and fled.

Naomi tripped on a chair and went down hard on her knees and I stopped to help her up. The boom of a gunshot cut off the crazy cackling laugh behind me. I pulled Naomi off the floor and kept going without looking back.

My throat pounded and burned at the same time and I stopped in the stairwell, leaning over with my hands on my thighs. A high-pitched whine filled my ears, and I grabbed for the iron railing, steadying myself while I caught my breath.

"We have to get out of here," I said, meeting Naomi's gaze. She glanced at the ceiling and then nodded. Valerie crossed my mind too, but we didn't have the luxury of a rescue mission. If we tried, it would put her right in the path of danger.

Another gunshot rang out, and I caught my breath, blowing out a stream of air before straightening just as a scream pierced the air.

"Time to go, now," I said and took her hand. We vaulted up the stairs and stepped into the back of the emergency room. Into a world of chaos.

We sidestepped out of the way as a group of officers ran by and my gaze landed on the unattended truck. My hand slid into my front pocket and the metal of the spare key ring sent a jolt through my form that moved me forward.

Demon nurse was nowhere to be seen, and I helped Naomi into the front seat and crossed to the driver's side. Ignoring the red stain on the seat and the stench of blood in the small space, I threw the car in gear and peeled out, heading away as fast as possible. I expected to be followed, especially when I was driving like the truck was my Aston Martin and I was on the Audubon.

Naomi gagged, and I glanced at her. "Open the window, it might help," I said and then focused back on the road. I knew the car had markings, so we were untraceable to celestial beings. I wasn't sure about demons or whatever else was out there.

I didn't truly exhale until we were in the dark garage and the door had dropped the last inch and the whine of the motor above shut off. I climbed out of the vehicle and made it to the kitchen sink in time to feel the bile burn the back of my throat. The cold water I splashed on my face didn't stop the onset of the shakes.

For a man who had dealt in death for so many years, this reaction rocked me to the core and I crossed to the table on shaking legs. Naomi was already sitting with her arms crossed on the walnut finish and her face buried in the crook of her elbow. Silent sobs shook her form, and I ran my damp hand over her back, not speaking for fear of splitting into a million pieces.

My phone buzzed, and I pulled it out, staring at the number.

"Fuck," the word spit out, interrupting Naomi's outburst. She stiffened under my hand and lifted her tear-stained face.

I pressed the button and put the phone to my ear.

"I will find you," Lucifer's voice growled on the line.

"I'll be ready when you do." I clicked the off button and put the phone down, shocked at how calm and cold I sounded. My hand continued the slow caress over Naomi's back as I stared out the windows at the beginning signs of spring.

"Who was that?"

I pressed my lips together and flipped the phone over, showing her the display with Valerie's number as the last call received. I couldn't speak yet; I was still dealing with an internal storm that threatened to become a hurricane.

Naomi leaned into me, laying her head on my shoulder. I wrapped my arm around her and set the phone back on the table. Every muscle in my form pounded with the same dull ache that overtook my head. Too much had happened in such a short time and I was still numb.

"I need to call Ted," I said, avoiding most of the swirl inside me. I stood, but Naomi increased her hold on me.

"Don't shut down," she said.

My gaze moved from the backyard to her deep brown eyes.

I couldn't help the laugh that bubbled up, and I peeled her off me, pulling away because with the laughter came a violent anger and I didn't want it aimed at her. The tidal wave swept through me and I clenched my fists, trying to contain the fury and the need to destroy.

Instead of addressing her comment, I stormed away, heading down into the basement. By the time I hit the tunnel, I was in a sprint, trying to run from the emotions wrestling for dominance. The trap door to the garage nearly peeled away from the hinges when I slammed it open and I climbed into the garage, with my chest heaving.

I let out a roar and picked up the closest thing, a socket wrench, and whipped it across the garage. The clang of metal on concrete just fueled my rage. A crow bar was next, but this time I turned, swinging it like I was hitting a grand slam. When the curved edge struck the side of my Ford 150, the satisfying give of metal reverberated up the shaft and into my arms. I didn't stop there. Twenty-five hundred years of fury blew and I beat the truck over and over and over, ignoring the shatter of glass and creak of metal until my arms were too tired to swing anymore.

I stumbled back into the wall, letting the crow bar fall to the floor before I sank to the ground. I folded my arms on my knees and rested my head against them before the sobs overtook me. The rips coming from my chest echoed in the garage, sounding more like an animal than a human.

I don't know how long I sat there sobbing. Time just seemed to fold in on itself and it wasn't until her hand touched the back of my head that I noticed more than just myself. The soft caress of her fingers through my hair silenced me, but they didn't stop the tears and I didn't look up. Shards of glass and metal sprinkled the floor within my vision and I focused on the prisms of light each piece represented through the sheen of my tears.

Her soft coo repeated in time with her fingers and when I raised my head and met her gaze, her bloodshot eyes told me I wasn't the only one experiencing this profound sadness. In silence, I pulled her into my arms and just held her, looking beyond her at the annihilated vehicle.

When I finally let her go, she turned and looked at my destruction.

"At least it wasn't the Aston-Martin," she said.

A smile surfaced. "Luckily, it wasn't the closest vehicle to the opening," I said, my voice raw from my outburst.

"Feel better now?" Naomi asked and wiped my cheeks.

I took a deep breath and exhaled before climbing to my feet and helping her up. I didn't quite know how to answer that question, because, while the fury was gone, a fire still burned in the middle of my chest.

"I'm not going to destroy anything else." I crossed to the closet and pulled out the broom, taking my time cleaning up the mess I made. Naomi took a seat on the stool lining my workbench, and her eyes tracked my movement.

"Imagine if I still had my vampire strength?" I said as I scooped up the first of many debris-filled dustpans and dumped it into the garbage bin.

Her quick laugh echoed, and I met her gaze.

"No, I can't imagine," Naomi said, her eyes still glistening with a sheen of tears. "You ready to talk?"

What was it with women and talking? I stopped mid-sweep and stared at her, weighing my reaction. "There really isn't anything to discuss," I said.

Her eyebrows curved, and her gaze dropped to the remaining pieces of the car. It was her *I-beg-to-differ* look, and I ignored it, returning to my task of cleaning up the mess I created.

She huffed and jumped off the chair, heading for the exit.

"Naomi," I said a little too sharply, and she spun.

"What?"

"I'm trying," I started, and leaned my forehead on the broomstick, pushing the flood waters back down into the well of my soul. "I just need to figure out what the hell is going on inside me before I'll be able to articulate it, okay?"

Her silence brought my gaze from the floor to her face. She gave me a strained smile and nodded before leaving me to finish what I started.

Trinity Rising
Chapter Five
Damian

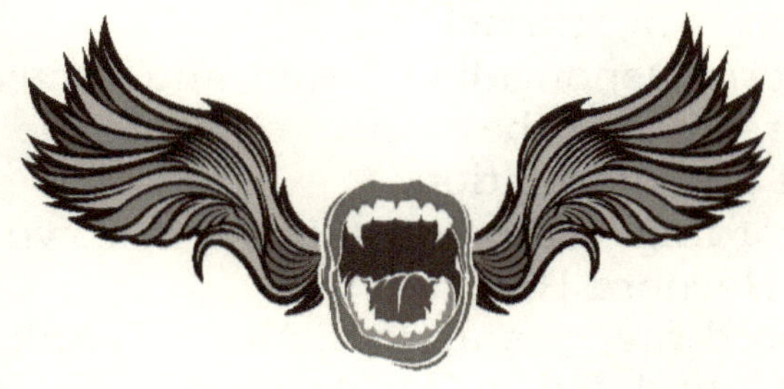

I FOUND NAOMI IN our bedroom, curled up on the bed with a throw blanket covering her. I leaned against the doorjamb, crossing my arms, and contemplated whether or not to interrupt her sleep. Her soft snore permeated through the fringe of the blanket and I sighed, stepping out of the room. She needed rest, and I had a phone call to make.

My stomach growled, and I diverted from the table to the refrigerator, opening it and scanning the contents. Nothing appealed to me and I closed the door, stepping back to the table and my cell phone.

The thought of calling Valerie's uncle left my chest tight, and I opted to call the hospital to find out how she was instead.

"Charlotte Hungerford Hospital. How may I help you?"

"I understand my cousin was brought into the emergency room earlier today," I started. "The last information I was given was that she was in surgery. Can you tell me what her status is now?"

"What is her name?"

"Valerie Denongalis," I said and waited while the person on the other end of the phone entered the information.

"According to the notes, she was flown by Life Star to Hartford Hospital."

I closed my eyes and exhaled. "Thank you." I hung up and did a Google search, finding the number to Hartford Hospital, and repeated the process.

They took down my name and phone number, validating I was on the list of next of kin. Once they were satisfied, they put me on hold. I paced while waiting for a voice, glancing at the clock and calculating the time we first entered the emergency room and now. Seven hours had passed. A hell of a lot more than I thought, and the longer I was on hold, the more unnerved I got.

"Mr. Andreas?" a male voice asked.

"Yes."

"I'm Dr. Browne, the surgeon in charge of your cousin's case," he said and papers shuffled. "She is in the recovery room at the moment, but we will move her to the intensive care within the hour."

"Is she... okay?"

The doctor hesitated. "I'll know more in the morning. I understand her uncle is on the way.

If you have the means to get here..." he drifted off.

"Unfortunately, I'm not in the position to get to Hartford at the moment," I said. "Can you give me some specifics?"

"The knife punctured her right kidney, and we were unable to save it. It also nicked the renal artery, and she lost a great deal of blood."

"She can survive with one kidney, right?"

"Yes, the kidney is the least of her worries," the doctor said. "The blood loss and increased chance of infection are the bigger issues, but now that we've contained the bleeding, she should have a better chance of fighting off whatever bacteria might have been on that knife."

I remained quiet. "Chances of survival?" I asked when he said nothing more.

"If she makes it through the night, I can give you better odds."

"What are her odds of making it through the night?"

"A little better than fifty percent."

"Thank you. I appreciate the information," I said and hung up. My next call was to Ted, and it took a couple of rings before he answered.

"Damian?" he asked after the shuffle sounds stopped.

"Yes, sir."

"I assume you know what happened," he said. A blinker sounded in the background.

"Demons, sir," I said. "They attacked her when we were in Torrington."

"What the hell were you doing in Torrington?"

"Valerie wanted Naomi checked out by a doctor."

"Why?"

"Naomi is pregnant."

Silence. Ted's breathing filled the line and all the prophecies Michael had told came to the forefront of my mind.

"Naomi's due in October and Val was worried that she might be diabetic." I crossed the kitchen and leaned on the window frame, scanning the wood line beyond the fence. "Val took us to the doctor's office."

"Let me guess, the doctor was a demon?"

I blinked at the venom in his question. "No. One of the nurses."

"You think that's a coincidence?"

"I... uh," I stumbled on the words.

"They've been watching the house ever since Michael dropped the two of you on our doorstep, and you can bet they were laying in wait for this day."

The mention of Michael's name tightened my throat. "Michael's dead."

"What?"

"Lucifer showed up at the hospital. So did Michael, and he didn't make it." Just recounting the day sucked the life out of me and I walked to the couch in the living room, dropping into the soft cushions. "I don't know how soon after that they sent Val to Hartford, but I'm glad they did, otherwise Lucifer would have found her and eaten her heart, too."

"How did you get out of there?"

"Cops converged." It was the first time in my life I had been truly happy to see a cop in the vicinity. "And I grabbed Naomi and ran." I paused and licked my lips. "Did you know Michael gave me his grace?"

An exhale filled the line. "No. He didn't mention that, but I knew bringing you back from the dead nearly did him in," Ted said, and the soft purr of the engine cut off. "I'm at the hospital. I'll let you know if her condition changes."

"Thank you."

"And Damian?"

"Yeah?"

"You and Naomi need to look for another place to live."

I huffed a laugh out. "What?"

"I have to keep my niece safe, and I can't with you there."

"Ted..." I trailed off. He was right, and even though the property was mine, it was where Valerie had lived all her life. I couldn't take that away from her, not when association with me had cost her everything else.

"I'm serious. I want the two of you gone before I bring her home from the hospital."

There was no leeway in his statement, and I closed my eyes. "Fine. I'll start looking in the morning."

"I'll let you know if anything changes with Valerie," he said and hung up the phone.

I dropped the phone on the table and rubbed my face. Naomi wasn't going to take this well, and I had no clue how I'd get us out of here without being attacked.

NAOMI STEPPED INTO THE room in the middle of a yawn. I did a quick glance at her and then focused back on my computer without a word. There were so many options on where we could go that I was at an impasse.

"Where do you want to live?" I finally asked, looking up as she took a seat on the couch.

"Here."

"Not an option."

"Damian..."

"Ted wants us gone before he brings Valerie home," I cut her off and glanced back at the computer. "And I have no idea where you want to live." I returned my gaze to her. "New York is not an option," I added before she fell back on her usual location.

"What do you mean, Ted wants us to go?"

I leaned back and kept her stare. I didn't need to speak, either. It was obvious after today. Anyone close to us would always be in danger, and I dropped my gaze to her stomach before looking back at the computer.

My children would always be on the run.

The reality of that statement shot me to my feet, and I crossed, slipping outside onto the patio and into the chill of the falling evening. I longed for the simplicity of life. The cluelessness of not knowing angels or demons or things much darker existed. I wanted a normal life for my children, not this hide to survive bullshit.

I glanced up at the stars and sighed. Maybe it was time to go home.

Naomi stepped next to me, glancing up at the stars in the twilight sky.

"What about Greece?" I said, still scanning the deepening colors of dusk.

The way she sighed pulled my attention to her. She looked between the sky and my face before turning toward me.

"While I'd love to see Greece at some time, this country is my home."

I knew she'd say that and as much as I longed for the white beaches and azure water of my birthplace; I hadn't been back, and I didn't know if it would be the same.

"I can't talk you into some place like Australia or New Zealand?"

She hesitated, studying the colorful sky before she spoke. "Again, those are places I'd like to visit, but I just can't see living there. And before you ask, the same goes for South America and Africa. I love my country. I don't want the devil chasing me out of my home."

"The west coast?"

"California isn't my style either. I enjoy having the seasons."

"Tahoe has seasons," I said, but her head was shaking. "We already did the mountains and while I loved Colorado, I missed home."

"That leaves Alaska or Hawaii," I said, thinking of places as far away from here as possible.

She laughed and met my gaze with a shake of her head.

She wasn't giving me much of the landscape to work with. "Somehow, I can't see you in the south either," I said and gave her a hint of a smile.

Naomi's dimples made an appearance. "You can't see me saying y'all?"

"No, no, I can't," I actually chuckled and pulled her to me. "You definitely are not a mild-mannered southern belle. I can see you as a kick-ass cowgirl, though."

She wrinkled her nose at me and shook her head. "I'm not interested in the wild west."

I tilted my chin toward my chest and raised an eyebrow. "Then where?"

She bit her lip. "Have you ever been to…" She paused and glanced up at the stars. "…Maine?"

I followed her gaze. "It's still too close."

"Have you ever been there?"

I shook my head. That was one state I hadn't been to and the idea of still being in New England didn't sit well with me. Being on this half of the world didn't sit well, but I knew I'd never get Naomi to agree to raise children on a deserted island in the South Pacific.

Hell, Lilith found us in the mountains of Colorado, so really, there wasn't any place safe on Earth and we damn well couldn't populate the moon.

I sighed. "Okay."

"Really?"

I dropped my gaze to hers. "Really. But I have to make it look like we are leaving the country." I planted a kiss on her forehead and led us back inside.

"I'm booking us on as many flights to Greece as I can from airports around here and in Michigan."

"Why Michigan?"

"I own one of the top automobile museums in the country. I'll send most of the car collection to them so they don't rot here."

"I didn't realize you had more than what's in the garage?"

"There are a lot of things you still don't know about me." I sent a grin her way and refocused. "I'm also going to book one flight out of Louisiana."

"Louisiana?"

"It's part of the shell game and he'll assume that's where we settled."

"New Orleans?"

I grinned and nodded.

"Isn't that a bit... cliché?"

"Absolutely, but he won't get it," I said and slid onto the couch. It took me close to an hour to book ten separate flights, ranging from as early as the following week out of Boston to the latest from Louisiana next month. The only flights that didn't have connections in the U.S. originated out of Boston, the rest of the flights had connections in O'Hare, Dulles or Atlanta.

When I finished, I cracked my knuckles and stretched my fingers before switching gears. I sent a note to the museum curator informing him I had a dozen more vehicles coming the following week, including pieces from ancient Greece and Rome. The response came in less than five minutes after I hit send, and I swear the man must have been close to a fucking orgasm with how much he gushed.

I sent a note back saying the vehicles needed some engine work because they had been sitting for most of the last five years, and he assured me they would be attended to when they arrived.

Next, I arranged for transportation of everything except my Aston-Martin; that would go wherever we went. The next couple of days would be busy loading vehicles and when I was done with the arrangements, I turned the computer to Naomi.

"Your turn. You need to look for a place for us to stay," I said and stood up. "I'm going to make sure I have everything I need to finish up the Aston Martin and hide it from view."

"Do I have a budget?" she asked as she pulled the computer onto her lap.

"Find a lease for now."

Disappointment transitioned her mouth into a pouty frown and I turned, leaving her to the task. I found my way through the underground tunnel and stood in the center of the garage, looking at the contents. The dozen vehicles, including the ornate chariots, would be gone by the end of the following day, and the rest of the things needed to be cleared out before we left. The Aston-Martin didn't have a great deal of storage space, so anything I wanted to come with us had to be compact.

I slid into the seat and turned the ignition key. The car jumped to life, purring like she should. All the work I had done over the past month had gotten her into shape and there wasn't anything I could think of that she needed. Even the tires had been replaced. I shut the car off and popped the trunk. I packed a toolbox with the wrench set and all the custom sockets I had for the different engine parts.

When I had everything I needed for future servicing, I closed the lid and placed the toolbox in the trunk, along with the extra oil filters and spark plugs for the car.

I cleared a space in the far right corner and pulled the car as close to the wall as I dared before putting a fitted cover over the vehicle. Then I moved boxes, old tires and two rolling tool chests I had around the car, hiding it from view and giving us the room to maneuver the rest of the vehicles.

I stepped back, scanning the area. It needed more, and I glanced at the ruined truck. Once I found the key, I yanked on the driver's door, but it didn't budge, so I climbed up on the bent foot rail and hauled myself through the empty window.

Despite my skepticism, the truck started, and I moved it, so it blocked the box barricade. I exited the way I entered and walked around to the belly of the garage. The mangled form did a better job of blocking the Aston Martin than the boxes and tool chests. Now it just looked like a normal garage storage space, along with a truck that needed serious bodywork.

Satisfied, I wiped my hands on my jeans and headed back to the house.

"York," Naomi said when I entered the living room.

I raised an eyebrow. "I told you, New York is not an option."

"No, York, Maine. It's a beach community, and I found a couple of rentals that would be perfect and they aren't outrageous."

She spun the computer toward me and I scanned the list of year-round rentals. They weren't bad and a few of the home rentals were downright beautiful. "Where is York?" I asked, hoping she'd say as far north as possible.

"It's like fifteen minutes from Portsmouth, New Hampshire."

I met her gaze and she wet her lips with her tongue and flashed that pleading smile that made it impossible to say no. Fuck it. I tapped the more expensive of the two condo rentals. "See if that's still available."

She picked up the phone, and I crossed into the kitchen to figure out something for dinner. We hadn't eaten much today, and I got that lightheaded feeling that comes with forgetting to eat. Instead of opting for some heavy Greek dish, I went simple and opened a can of tomato soup.

Naomi stepped into the kitchen behind me and wrapped her arms around my waist. Just the feel of her made my heart flutter, despite the day from hell, and I turned my head, catching a quick kiss over my shoulder.

"Do you want grilled cheese with this?"

She glanced at the stove and nodded. "I'll probably only have grilled cheese."

"Keeping it light?"

"Yeah, my stomach is still unsettled and not eating today didn't help."

I just nodded and continued stirring. Now that I wasn't actively doing anything, my mind started wondering about what Michael said today.

"Why did Michael give me his grace?" I asked with my back to Naomi. "And what the hell did he mean by now all I need is Lucifer's?" I didn't expect an answer and when Naomi didn't speak, I took a glance over my shoulder. She stood looking out the back window, her profile carved in thought.

I let it go, focusing back on our dinner. When I set our plates on the table, she turned and sighed, taking the seat opposite me. I brought two bowls and spoons along with the soup pot, just in case she changed her mind.

The minute I set the soup down, she turned ravenous, like she hadn't eaten in years. I had the forethought to make her two sandwiches, and she decided halfway through the first half to add soup to her meal.

"Maybe he's setting you up to be a true trinity." Naomi said around a mouthful of grilled cheese.

"How?"

"Maybe when your father died, you got his grace too."

I burst out laughing. "I still can't get over the fact I was the beneficiary of one angel's grace. I'm certainly not worthy of two."

Naomi's brow knit together and she took another bite of her sandwich. "Why do you do that?" Her eyes flared to match the sharpness in her tone.

"Sweetheart, I killed my fair share of people and some of them did not deserve to die. I'm not worthy of grace."

Her gaze narrowed. "Worthy or not, it sounds like you have it and you need to figure out how to use it."

My hands dropped to the table, and I stared at her. "What do you mean?"

"I might be wrong, but I have a feeling he could have made you better without granting you his grace."

This wasn't an idea I wanted to entertain. I didn't understand why Michael would be so foolish as to put himself in harm's way for me. "So he died for me?" I asked, my voice carrying all the incredulousness that filled my brain.

"Angels don't die, Damian. They just don't get to leave heaven anymore."

"Isn't that the same thing?" I asked her, leaning back in the chair and crossing my arms.

Her gaze turned to a glare. "That isn't the point. There was a reason Michael gave you his grace. We just need to figure it out, and I think his statement may have been the key."

"Look, right now, I want to get us as far from this house as I possibly can. I want you and my child to be safe, and the last thing I want to do is confront Lucifer. You saw just as much as I did. He's almost back to full strength, which means if we cross his path, we have nothing to defend ourselves with."

"There has to be a way to kill that bastard," she said.

"Okay, I'm curious, now that we're human, just how in the hell do you suggest we kill an angel?" I countered, leaning forward on the table because I really had no clue and wanted to hear what she had to say. After all, she had nearly done him in when she was a vampire in tiger form.

"You steal his grace," she said like it was an achievable thing.

I started laughing. "You are out of your fucking mind."

Naomi huffed and pushed her plate in, crossing her arms in that stubborn manner that made me want to take her over my knee. Anger bloomed, and I stood, clearing the table before I said something I'd regret.

"I'm serious."

I spun from the sink. "You had the strength to kill him when you were a vampire; I never had that kind of power."

She stood and cut the distance between us to nothing but a fraction of an inch. "You're the stronger one now."

Her hand landed on my chest, and I stared into her eyes. Into the conviction displayed in her deep chocolate irises and laughed. I looked up at the ceiling, cursing my bloodline as well as hers. I turned away from her, finishing the dishes instead of continuing this insane conversation.

"Have you heard anything more about Valerie?"

I wiped my hands on a dishtowel, realizing that I hadn't told her about the conversation I had with the doctor. "I talked to her doctor before I called Ted. Life Star took Valerie to Hartford Hospital once she stabilized enough to travel. Her doctor said they had to remove her right kidney and they could give us a better idea of her recuperation time in the morning." I left out the fact her odds weren't ideal for making it through the night. Naomi didn't need to know just how close we came to losing her. "And Ted said he'd call me if anything changed."

Naomi just stared at me, her eyelashes batting like she didn't quite understand. "They flew her to Hartford?"

"Yes. She needed a trauma one center, and that's the closest one. If they hadn't, she probably would have died from blood loss." Instead of taking a seat at the table, I left the kitchen and flopped on the couch, turning the laptop towards me. I hadn't logged into the day job at all and when I opened my business email account, I exhaled at the flurry of activity.

The last piece of the shell game needed to be addressed, and I sent a note to my boss, telling him I needed some personal time in order to move. He must have been online because my phone buzzed and I glanced at Naomi.

"What do you mean, you need more time off?" Kevin bellowed in my ear when I answered.

"It's either that or I'll have to give notice," I said and pinched the bridge of my nose to dull the forming headache.

"You're the best damn programmer I have and we need you," he pushed. "The project will not get done in time if you leave."

"Kevin, I'm not in a position to give you a whole hell of a lot of time right now. If you can live with what I can give, when I can give it, then we're good. Otherwise..." I trailed off, trying not to get aggravated with him. I knew I was putting him in a difficult spot, but I just couldn't see a way around it. Juggling everything I had in the air right now needed my concentration, otherwise, I'd screw up.

As trite as it sounded, lives were at stake, and failing was not an option.

A project timeline put in jeopardy just seemed so ridiculously unimportant in comparison, but I didn't want to burn any bridges.

A huff came over the line and I could just imagine him chewing on his lip while overlooking some concrete landscape out the window. He exhaled. "What can you give me?"

I closed my eyes and dropped my chin to my chest. Whatever I promised, I'd have to follow through on, no matter what, and right now that was a nearly impossible commitment. Instead of saying I couldn't give him anything, I said, "I can commit to five hours a week for the next month."

"An hour a day? Are you fucking kidding me?"

"It's what I can commit to. If I find I can give you more, I will."

"Does this have anything to do with the accident?"

My eyes opened, and I met Naomi's gaze. That was the excuse she gave when I was in a coma. A car accident. I wish it had been that instead of Lucifer playing tic-tac-toe on my chest with a razor, or beating me to a pulp with his fist. An accident would have been cleaner and easier to deal with. Instead, I had nightmares every night and now I had to face that bastard again.

"Damian?"

"Yes, there have been some complications that need to be addressed," I answered and just left it at that.

"Are you... okay?" he asked in a voice softened with concern.

"I'm not dying, if that's what you're worried about," I said.

"Oh, okay, that's good," Kevin said, stumbling before he recovered his authoritative boom. "I guess we can work around your schedule," he added.

"Thank you."

"Can you look at the issue the testers found?"

"Yeah, I'll take a look now and shoot over my findings in a few," I said and disconnected the call. "Shit." The last thing I wanted to do was work.

Naomi stretched out on the couch next to me, using my thigh as a pillow. She flipped on the television while I shuffled through the email chain.

After a few minutes, the irony of the situation hit me and I chuckled.

Naomi glanced up at me with her brow scrunched in her what-the-fuck look.

"For someone who's supposed to save the world, being stuck troubleshooting code is completely fucked up."

Dimples appeared even before her giggle and she rolled her eyes, settling back down on my lap to catch the rest of the show.

I had the problem figured out and fixed before the half-hour sitcom ended and sent a note to my boss. I folded the laptop, set it on the table, and stretched.

"Are we all set with that condo?" I asked, and Naomi rolled onto her back, looking straight up at me.

"They weren't there when I called and they haven't called back yet."

"If it doesn't pan out, we can always stay at a hotel until we find something." I cupped her cheek and ran my thumb over her lips, enjoying the silkiness of her skin.

"When are we leaving?"

"Your guess is as good as mine." I shifted and brushed her hair away from her face, tucking the stray hairs behind her ear. "It won't be until after all the cars are on their way to Michigan and we may have to stay downstairs for a few days. Just until I think it's clear to go."

She raised an eyebrow.

"Besides, I have to reprogram the access to the rooms downstairs. I need to make a failsafe that will freeze the lock if someone attempts to override the commands I put in place. I don't want anyone getting in or out of there after we go. I want to make it so they'd have to blast the door off with dynamite to gain access."

"Why?"

"I'm not worried about Ted and Valerie using the place. I'm more concerned with someone finding their way in from the garage." I shrugged, leaving the possibilities open, and she slowly nodded. "Demon's can't get past the entry pipe—but anything else can."

"If you lock it up..." she started, and I raised my eyebrows at her, silently telling her to rethink the statement before she continued. Naomi inhaled and nodded, getting my point.

"I want to leave the garage open. That way, they'll know it's empty and that we've left for good. But before we go, not only do I have to do the reprogramming magic, I also need to solder the door at the bottom of the stairs and do the same to the hatchway so nothing can get through. And, just for good measure, I'll move the truck over the hatch to make it less obvious. Once we're in Maine, I'll make sure the ownership of both the property and the garage is transferred to Valerie and she can do whatever she wants with it."

Leaving unnoticed would not be easy, but if I could pull it off, it would give us time. How much time was the question, and I broke eye contact with Naomi, looking out at the dark settling over the backyard.

If I didn't succeed at this, God only knew what the hell we'd unleash.

Naomi yawned and stretched, pulling my attention away from the outside world, and I smiled down at her. I wish I knew what she was thinking. I missed the mind reading abilities we shared as vampires and I sighed, running my fingertips over her sexy lips.

She grabbed my wrist and pulled my index finger into her mouth. Heat stirred inside me and I closed my eyes for a moment as she slowly released it. When she teased me like this, I could feel the fire between us burn bright. I opened my eyes and allowed the slow grin she adored to form.

It had the desired effect; she propped herself up to meet my hungry lips.

Her mouth tasted like caramel, and she wrapped her arms around my neck, deepening the kiss. Her tongue danced slowly with mine, turning off logical thought. The animal in me reared up, carnal and wanting, and I wrapped my arms around her, pulling her closer.

A distant buzz cut through my lust and I pulled away from her sweet lips, meeting her gaze before transitioning my attention to the phone on the table. It could be Ted and I sighed, pushing her aside and picked up the phone.

Any heat she'd created turned to an icy fury at the caller ID and every muscle tensed into hard knots. I inhaled, closing my eyes before bringing the phone to my ear.

His malignant chuckle drifted over the line.

"What the fuck do you want?" I growled into the phone through clenched teeth. I opened my eyes, meeting Naomi's gaze.

"I want your wife and your unborn child."

"Not on your life."

"My plans have changed a bit since you seemed to have already created the first pure trinity. I'll gladly trade your daughter's soul for your wife's. I can't think of anything more perfect than deflowering a virgin trinity. If you deliver Naomi to me, I'll let you live to watch your daughter grow and become my concubine," he purred, pushing dangerous buttons.

"You must be pretty bad off to think I'd entertain the idea of a negotiation. Why don't we make a deal? You leave us the fuck alone and I won't kill you," I said, and Naomi shivered in my arms. Before he could interject some more horrifying images, I continued, "Did you know when an angel dies, they get locked in heaven? I wonder what happens when the devil dies?"

Naomi's eyes widened, and she shook her head.

In the back of my mind, I wondered why the hell I was poking a sleeping dragon, but for the first time, I seemed in control of the conversation and it gave me the audacity to taunt him.

"I am going to enjoy watching you die," Lucifer growled, pulling a smile from within my anger.

"Yeah, I've heard that before. At least three times, but it doesn't seem to stick, now does it?" I asked and winked at Naomi, enjoying this more than I should.

A roar came over the line. "I'll kill you both, you little shit!"

"You will never get the chance."

"I will hunt you down and rip your heart out," he growled.

"You're such a sadistic bastard, you know that?" I laughed, realizing somewhere along the way the tides had turned in my favor.

"You think you can hide in Greece?" he asked, his voice barely steady.

"It's a big world, my friend, and who knows, maybe I'll organize me a demonic hunting party. I really enjoy killing those bastards and I'm sure eventually the path of dead assholes will lead me to you."

"Damian," Naomi whispered, and I met her panicked gaze. I smiled and palmed her cheek.

"Now, if you don't mind, I'm going to make love to my wife," I said and cut the call, tossing the phone onto the table.

"Are you out of your fucking mind?"

I raised my eyebrow at her outburst. "What?"

"Do you really think pissing off Lucifer is a smart idea?"

"You know what? I've been walking on eggshells for twenty-five hundred years trying not to piss off the legion of angels, and what has it gotten me? I'm done. I'm not taking shit from any of them ever again." I stood, pulling her to her feet and shutting off her argument with my lips.

Fired up was an understatement, and I focused all the built up frustration on her. I swept her up into my arms and turned off the lights, carrying her to our bedroom.

Trinity Rising
Chapter Six
Naomi

THE ICY FIRE IN his eyes, along with the determined set of his jaw, jumpstarted my heart, spreading a flush over my skin, and I shivered with anticipation. Even with the shitty day we've had and the insane call from Lucifer, one hungry gaze from Damian still sent me into the land of lust.

When he laid me out on the bed, I stared at him, taking in his hard form from head to toe as he stripped. Without clothing, the man screamed perfection, and I caught the twinkle in his eyes as he crawled toward me.

Damian licked his lips and pushed my shirt up, finding my skin with his hot tongue. The magic in his fingertips sent me into orbit and he started unbuttoning my pants and then stripped away every stitch of fabric. A side of him I had never seen came out tonight.

Rough, demanding, in control and hotter than hell.

The things he did to me were far from the gentle, thoughtful lover I spent the last five years with. I think he even growled at one point, nipping and stroking with such abandon that I got lost between the pleasure and pain.

He claimed my body with a vengeance that left me breathless, filling me with a need so palpable that our room filled with steam.

I don't know how long we went at it, but when it was over, we lay side by side staring at the ceiling, both of us panting for breath. I turned my head and met his satiated gaze. He gave me that one dimple smile that warmed my form and I sent one back, still unable to speak.

My body felt supple and exhausted, exhilarated and thrilled all at the same time. My muscles trembled from exertion and I closed my eyes.

"Damn, boy," I finally said with a breathless sigh.

He chuckled and rolled on his side, pulling me into him.

"I love you, Naomi," he whispered in my ear with a voice as ragged as my own.

"I love you, too," I said and turned so I could accept a kiss. As tired as I was, I couldn't fall asleep, even when his breathing slowed into that soft cadence of sleep.

Being human had changed Damian in more ways than I think he knew. He still had a kind heart, but he now had command over his emotions. They no longer broadcast in his every expression. Most notably, the haunted look that had been in his eyes since I first met him was no longer there.

We've always had an active sex life. Sometimes it got wild, and when we were both vampires, it included sinking our teeth in each other's throat at the moment of orgasm. But even those wild nights paled compared to this.

Not once in our courtship had he ravaged me like he did tonight.

I shifted in his arms and his breathing hitched and then smoothed out. Gently, I moved his hand and rolled out of bed as a different need struck. I made my way into the bathroom, did my business, and stopped at the sink. My hair looked like a bird's nest and I took time to brush it before heading back to bed.

On my way through the bedroom, something in the dark caught my attention, and I crossed to the window, squinting into the darkness. A small spark erupted at the closest point of the fence and I gasped at the face illuminated by a lighter. My arms crossed over my bare breasts and Lucifer took a long drag and blew a stream of smoke into the air, sending the most disturbing smile my way before the flame extinguished, leaving only the glow of the cigarette in the darkness.

I stepped farther into the shadows and swallowed the vile taste of fear.

Damian sat up in bed, staring at me, and our eyes locked. The smile on his face froze my heart in place. It was the same one Lucifer wore just before the lighter went out.

"What's wrong, baby, you don't like dancing with the devil?" he asked in a way that left me frigid. It was Damian's voice, but it was *not* my husband.

A SCREAM PEELED FROM my throat, burning it raw with the force and the nightstand light switched on.

"Naomi?" his hand caressed my arm, and I cranked my head in his direction.

I sat stalk straight in the bed; the covers knotted around me, and his sleepy, worried gaze met mine. It took a full minute to get my breathing under control and I blinked in confusion at the nightmare. The bed trembled with the shakes racking my form, and Damian wrapped his arms around me, kissing my temple.

"Do you want to talk about it?" he asked and I couldn't help the hysterical laugh that came bubbling up.

Complete confusion overwhelmed me and I wondered if I had dreamed the entire night; but the ache in my hips and the pressure in my bladder told me otherwise. Still, I had to ask.

"Was... did..." I couldn't articulate, and I met Damian's gaze. "Did we..."

He grinned, and the blush heightened in his cheeks and then his smile faded, worry replacing it. "You thought that was part of your nightmare?"

My mouth opened to speak and then I closed it, wondering exactly what I was going to say.

"I... I'm sorry," he whispered, coming to the wrong conclusion.

"Don't apologize, you were...beyond fantastic, it's just, you've never been like that before," I started and saw a flare of hurt pass over his face. He shifted the covers and dropped his gaze.

"I dreamed Lucifer had somehow possessed you."

His eyes snapped to mine.

I offered a shrug in my defense. "And you were so... so different than you usually are that I thought—"

"Jesus," he muttered and ran his hands through his hair, the horror of it all reflecting on his face.

"Yeah, it was bizarre." I slipped out of bed, heading for the bathroom to relieve myself. I grabbed a nightgown on my way by the dresser to dilute the discomfort of being exposed. When I came back out, Damian had straightened the covers and sat with his arms crossed and that brooding expression that I immediately recognized.

He was getting more irritated by the second and he met my gaze when I slipped into the bed.

"How can you even think that?" he snapped, taking me by surprised.

"Look, in the dream I saw something out the window that caught my attention. It was Lucifer, and he was outside the fence smoking a cigarette like they do in the old movies, you know, after fucking around. And you, you sat up with that same shit-eating grin and asked me how I liked dancing with the devil."

Damian blinked, and his eyebrows rose.

"Then I woke up screaming."

Damian's gaze moved past me to the window and back, and the tightness in his jaw softened. "I can assure you, that was all me." He blushed.

"But Lucifer was the one who brought out the beast in you," I said.

His gaze dropped to his hands, and he took a deep breath as he analyzed my comment and his head started shaking back and forth. "No. Lucifer had nothing to do with my behavior tonight." He turned his glance toward me. "You had everything to do with it. I'll concede that my anger may have made me a bit more callous than usual, or less inhibited, but you're the one who drives me insane." A dimple appeared. "In the best way possible," he added.

Trinity Rising
Chapter Seven
Naomi

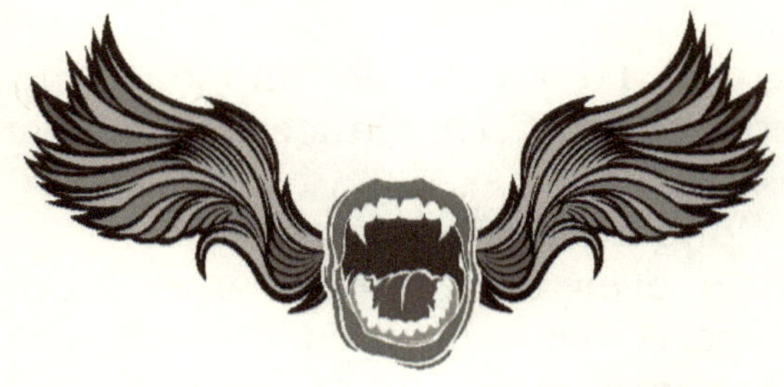

THE MORNING SUN DRENCHED the bedroom, and I blinked, rolling away from the open curtains. Damian's side of the bed was empty, and I pushed myself up into a sitting position. My stomach decided that wasn't the brightest thing to do, and I clamped my hand over my mouth, running to the bathroom as the bile crawled up my throat.

I did not like this side effect of pregnancy. Dealing with an unsettled stomach close to twenty-four hours a day sucked. Exhaustion I could deal with, but this, this was a royal pain. I spit in the toilet and climbed to my feet, flushing before washing the nasty taste from my mouth. I wrapped a warm bathrobe around my body and headed into the living room.

Damian looked up from his position on the couch, his computer propped on his lap and a pencil sticking out of both sides of his mouth.

Papers and a yellow pad lay across the couch and I smiled. He pulled the pencil from between his teeth.

"Hey, how are you feeling?"

"Eh. What are you doing?" I waved toward the mess.

"I figured I'd try to get most of the time I promised to Kevin." He glanced at his watch and stretched.

"How long have you been at it?"

"A little over three hours and I only have another forty-five minutes before the auto-transport company is due to arrive."

I glanced at the clock. "You got up at five?"

"I couldn't get back to sleep," he said, folding the computer and putting it on the table. He arranged the paperwork into a neat pile and then set it on top of his computer before he finally met my stare.

When he didn't offer an explanation, I shrugged and asked, "Why not?"

He stood and retreated to the kitchen, and I followed. After he popped a couple of pieces of bread into the toaster, he turned, leaning on the counter behind him.

"The more I thought about it, the angrier I got," he said.

My mouth went dry, and I wasn't sure I wanted to know, but I asked anyway. "Thought about what?"

"Everything." He didn't continue right away. Instead, he focused on buttering the toast and bringing it to the table, setting it in front of the chair I stood behind. "I'm pissed that we're pawns in their fucking game," he said and sat down.

The toast smelled good, and my mouth watered, so I took a bite. He yawned, covering it with his hand before continuing.

"I've been running for centuries, surviving by hiding away: from the sun, from Lucifer, even from Michael for a time. Every time I thought I found peace, the angels rained down on me, spoiling it in some manner. I will not let that happen this time."

The intensity in his eyes made me swallow hard.

"I'm done being afraid," he added and crossed his arms. "Death is just an end to the running and if I don't stop him this time, my child will never know peace."

An icy fear pierced my heart and spread through my body, almost doubling me over. I dropped the slice I held onto the plate. "I'm not letting you sacrifice yourself for us. I need you just as much as your child does."

He laughed in a way that sparked an irrational irritation.

"I'm not suggesting that I become a martyr, honey. I'm talking about killing him. Ending his reign of terror and walking away from it." He reached over and snatched one slice of toast. "You got me thinking. There has to be a way to kill an angel and with Lucifer, I'm not sure stealing his grace is achievable, but we both know he can be killed. You're the one who's got the closest to that goal, so I just need to figure out how to do it without the tiger."

"I almost beat him because he was in human form."

"We're both painfully aware of the differences between human and angel forms," he said with a sigh. "I think he's stuck in human form until he mends completely. At least that's what I'm hoping."

"He looked pretty whole after eating Michael's heart." My appetite vanished. Damian nodded and he exhaled audibly through his nose.

"I know. I guess I expected Michael to fight back in some way, even in his debilitated state."

"Yeah, I think I expected him to sprout wings and smite that bastard."

Damian let out a small laugh. "I should have taken advantage of the situation and attacked while he was still vulnerable." He met my gaze and shrugged. "I think that's the thing that pisses me off the most. That was probably the best chance I had of beating Lucifer and I ran away like a frightened little girl."

The venom in his voice gave me pause, and I searched his face for a moment. "You were protecting me."

He nodded. "You and the baby."

"And really, what could you have done with the cop there?"

"I could have broken his neck, like I did to that demon," he answered. "It would have at least slowed him down, and maybe he wouldn't have killed that cop."

I jerked with the shock of his statement. "He killed..." I started and trailed off.

"It was on the news this morning, along with my face. Plastered all over the fucking news. I'm apparently a person of interest," he said, using finger quotes around the words person of interest.

I blinked at him, and my eyebrows arched.

"They didn't have a clear picture of you," he said and offered a smile. "But they have one of me, looking shocked as shit."

Muscles I didn't realize I had tensed, relaxed a fraction. I don't look any different from five years ago and I'm sure if this story went national, some of my friends in New York might have been able to provide an identity that would be traced back to a dead girl.

"So, what else did they show?"

"Nothing. No footage of Lucifer, nothing, just my face, which looks like a still from a video feed, and a couple of seconds of us running as the cop yelled freeze."

I couldn't help the laugh that escaped, as if our lives weren't complicated enough. Now we had the police searching for us. My brain caught up, and I gasped, my gaze shooting back to Damian's. "They don't have footage of Lucifer?"

Damian slowly shook his head, and I exhaled, slumping in the chair. We needed a break, but it didn't look like it was coming any time soon.

"The bastard set us up."

I blinked, staring at him. "And he's using the media to find us."

"Bingo. Are you sure you don't want to go to Greece?" he asked, cocking his head. "Because right now, it looks like they're building a case against us."

"With your picture plastered all over the airwaves, there's no way we would get away with leaving the country," I said and he bit his bottom lip with an expression that agreed with my statement.

"The good news is not many people know my face and most of those people know me under an alias. There are only three people who know my name and address, and one is sitting right here."

"And the other two are at Hartford Hospital."

"Yes. I also spoke with Ted this morning. It looks like Valerie is going to be okay. She made it through the night without incident and she even regained consciousness enough to relay her version of the attack."

"Really?"

"Yes. Thankfully, that wasn't picked up by any news stories because Lucifer would put it together and go after her. At this point, he does not know where she went." Damian glanced at his watch and stood. "I have to go meet the auto-transport people." He paused at the doorway to the living room. "Just hang here, okay?"

The worry in his eyes made me nod. I didn't need to help pack the cars, anyway. I had some packing of my own to do. "Be careful," I said.

"I always am."

I huffed, and Damian rolled his eyes.

"I'll try," he added, and disappeared from view.

Trinity Rising
Chapter Eight
Naomi

I MADE THE MISTAKE of turning on the television and taking in the news story. The raw anger that bit at me sparked a chuff from my lips and the shock of the feral sound pulled my gaze to the floor, and the white-furred paws.

Shock transitioned through my body and I took another step, still locked in tiger form. I hissed and spat and padded down the stairs. The keypad was difficult to manage with my paw, but I finally had the idea of using one of my razor sharp nails.

The door squeaked open, and I padded my way down the tunnel, turning into a gallop and by the time I reached the stairs, my heart pounded and I was sure Damian was being tortured on the other side of the hatch. I flew up the stairs, using the strength in my massive shoulder to open the hatch. I came to a sliding stop in the middle of the garage, a snarl coming from my mouth.

Damian spun along with one of the work crew. I growled and then chuffed and licked my chops, looking between Damian and the group of workers who were backing away slowly. Their expressions would have made me laugh had I been in human form.

Damian gave me a cocked-head stare and then he approached, slowly.

"Hey, baby, how'd you get out of your cage?" he asked with a soft voice, like one meant to disarm an angry tiger.

"Wo, dude, that's yours?" one of the crew asked.

"Yeah, she's mostly harmless unless you decide to attack me or something," Damian said, coming up to me and running his hand over my head and scratching me behind the ear. I rubbed my head against his leg, knocking him back a step.

"Sit," he said with authority, and I glanced up at him. While I wanted to tell him to fuck off, I obeyed and sat down on my haunches before stretching my paws out.

"That's my girl," he said, and I actually bared my teeth at him for a moment before settling in place.

I wish I could have answered the questions in his eyes, but I didn't quite understand the switch, either. I was angry at the news story, but I had been angry before and never just popped into the tiger like this. It's usually caused by mortal danger, but there was no danger here.

I licked my paws as I watched them load car after car until all the vehicles were loaded. After Damian locked the doors, he turned and stared at me.

"What the fuck?" he asked.

I stood and stretched before crossing to him and rubbing against his leg.

He squatted and held my head between his hands. "Can you change back so we can talk?"

I licked his face, and he sat back on his haunches, concern marking his handsome face. The man smelled wonderful, and I stepped in, nuzzling against him.

"Naomi," he whispered, his voice carrying a warning, and I looked up at his face, but he wasn't looking at me anymore.

I turned my head and followed his gaze to the back door. Paws smashed through the door, breaking the hinges, and the door swung open. The stench of the thing made my nose crinkle. It smelled like a cross between a demon and a wet dog, and it didn't look much better.

The beast filled the exit, and I bared my teeth, positioning myself between this thing and Damian. The sound of metal scraping pulled my attention in Damian's direction and he stepped next to me. The crowbar gripped in his hand.

"What do you want?" Damian asked, like he expected the mutant dog to speak.

"I've been sent to bring your head back to my master," it growled and stepped inside.

The shock of actually hearing a hellhound talk gave me pause, and I measured it up against my formidable size. It wasn't as big as I was, and it certainly didn't have the raw strength I had. It looked more like a mangy mutt than a powerhouse.

It wasn't until the second one stepped in that my confidence wavered. The hatchway to the basement sat open, and I wondered what our chances were of making it to the tunnel opening. Although, I had doubts the salt ring would keep these demon-dogs out. Especially since I thought Damian had reinforced the garage.

The two split up, circling the outside edges, their growls echoing in the empty garage. I flexed my paws, bringing out my deadly claws. That was my advantage against the mangy beasts. They had teeth, but I had both teeth and claws and I tightened my muscles, getting ready to spring.

Damian raised the crowbar like a bat and turned his back toward me, covering me from that side. I focused on the beast closest to me and I didn't think either of them were aware of who I was, so another advantage. They were here to kill Damian, and right now, I stood in their way.

"Let's do this," Damian whispered, and I launched, twisted in the air, and landed on top of the mangy beast. My claws latched onto the dog's torso and I bit down on the back of its neck, hoping for a quick kill. It reared up and his howl of pain filled the garage. I shifted my nails, tearing at the beast's front chest. It tried to turn its head, but my jaws prevented him from reaching me. I ripped until blood started shooting and the thing stumbled to the ground. I shook it with a growl and then released, focusing on the one circling Damian.

The crowbar swung and connected with the beast's shoulder, but it got a piece of Damian's thigh with its teeth. Not enough to latch on, but enough to rip through jeans and flesh, drawing blood. With a roar, I launched. I hit the beast full on, my teeth clamping down on the underside of its throat, ripping through flesh and arteries in one powerful chomp. As we rolled, I raked my claws down its abdomen, tearing strips of flesh out, and then I was on my feet, ready for more. But both hellhounds were down, and Damian stood with the crowbar, waiting for another attack.

It took him a moment, but he looked between the two downed dogs and me.

"Holy shit," he muttered and took a step toward the door.

A flash darted from the door and I moved just as quickly, launching at the same moment the mutt launched at Damian. I caught it in the air and took it the same way I had the other one, quickly, efficiently and bloodily. I didn't let go until the beast's heart stopped and Damian spoke my name.

"Naomi."

I released, turning my attention to him. The taste of demon blood filled my mouth and the smell of death hung on the air.

I glanced toward the door and stepped away from the dead hellhound toward Damian. My paws were soaked red and I'm sure my white coat was sufficiently stained as well. After two paces, my view altered, and I looked down at bloody hands.

"I guess the danger has passed," I said, bringing my gaze back to Damian's wide eyes.

"How'd you know?"

"I didn't. One minute I was watching the news stories and the next I was the tiger. I thought I just changed because I got angry at the thinly veiled accusations on the television. They've even brought in some ex-FBI expert and you'll never guess where the hell he's from." I shifted, trying to make the pants I was wearing more comfortable, but I couldn't. Before Damian could venture a guess, I said, "I need a shower," and headed toward the hatchway.

Damian didn't follow me and I paused halfway down the tunnel, conflicted about going back until he was ready to come with me. The fact I was still human and not a carnivorous tiger clinched the decision. I continued to the downstairs bedroom and stripped when I stepped into the bathroom. The details in the marine mural still captivated me; stepping into the shower was like stepping into an underwater world of vibrant fish and coral reefs.

The water ran red for longer than I expected, even with scrubbing until my skin burned and my hair squeaked when I ran my fingers through it. When the water cleared, I closed my eyes and enjoyed the pummeling heat.

A breeze caressed my skin, creating goose flesh under the hot stream, and I opened my eyes. Damian stood naked in the doorway to the shower stall. His gaze slowly scanned my form, lingering on my breasts before traveling lower. A crease appeared between his eyes and his gaze bounced from my stomach to my face, locking with mine.

The question in his eyes made me drop my gaze to the bump in my belly. I had been so consumed with cleaning off the blood that I hadn't noticed the newly stretched skin. Bump was an understatement. Between the time I pulled on my pants this morning and now, I had popped and my gaze jumped back to his.

"Holy shit," he said and stepped under the spray with me, his hands finding the soft skin stretched over my abdomen. My gaze dropped to the red water running down his thigh and I turned him so I could inspect his wound.

"It's just superficial. Leave it be," he said, studying my belly with the same intensity that I gave the cut on his leg. When he lifted his gaze, there were a hundred unasked questions swirling in his vibrant irises, but I had no answer for him. I looked like someone who was at least six months pregnant and that explained why my pants were so damned uncomfortable when I transitioned back to human form.

"I know how long human incubation is, but how long is a tiger's?" he asked and I stared at him.

"You don't think..." I trailed off and the candor in his expression brought forth an unwelcomed shiver.

"It's not normal to grow this big overnight," he said, running his hands over my stomach. "And you did just change into a tigress." He smiled like he was not at all unsettled by this. "You know, you kicked ass like I've never seen," he added and drew me into a kiss.

I pushed him away, still too preoccupied with the tiger conclusion to get into a romantic tryst with him. "Damian," I said, and his eyes widened into that innocent look, followed by the brief appearance of his dimples.

"What?" He didn't suppress the smirk fast enough.

"This isn't funny," I said. "Do you think I did something bad to our child by changing?"

His smirk faded, and the first shadow passed over his gaze. He looked down at the symmetry under his hands. "No. I don't think you did something bad," he said, meeting my gaze. "We aren't normal, Naomi. To expect a normal pregnancy is asking for a lot, especially since this little bundle is a trinity." He patted my stomach, and I felt more than just a flutter. He pulled his hand away and then placed it back on my belly, awe painted on his features.

"The baby just kicked." He glanced up at me and grinned. "Did you feel it?"

Dumb question. I felt more than just a kick; I felt rotation, as if the child was moving. The sudden appearance of motion meant my child was alive, and I matched Damian's grin, nodding.

The worry was still present, but it dulled compared to the joy I felt. This time, when he pulled me into a kiss, I did not resist.

Trinity Rising
Chapter Nine
Naomi

I LAY IN BED, staring at the cloud-covered ceiling as Damian rested his ear on my stomach. He giggled a couple of times as a foot or hand passed over, connecting with his cheek.

"What if I give birth to some sort of hybrid?" I asked, voicing my growing concern.

He propped himself up on his elbow and offered a shrug. "We'll deal with it," he said.

"Aren't you the least bit worried?"

Damian sighed and shook his head. "No. Maybe I should be, but I'm not. It's..." He looked at the ceiling, his eyes moving around the room as he searched for the correct word. "Right," he finally said when his gaze locked on mine. "I know it's strange, but I can feel the rightness of this in my soul. Can't you?"

For the first time since I got the news, a strange calmness settled over me and I nodded. I felt the perfection of this situation just as much as he did. He smiled and studied me for a moment, his features adopting a more serious expression.

"Do you know what prompted you to change today?"

"No, at first I thought it was because I was frustrated by the speculation on the news. But then I couldn't just will myself back into human form. That's when I thought there might be an issue in the garage."

He huffed at me and pressed his lips to my stomach. "You've never had that issue before."

"No, but maybe the hormones are messing me up." That sounded like the most viable theory. It actually made sense, but who knows, it could be some divine intervention for all I knew.

"Do you think the hormones are giving you some level of precognitive ability? Sensing danger and forcing the tiger out?"

I laughed at his flawed logic. "I don't think so," I answered.

His eyebrow rose in a silent challenge.

"Then where the hell was the tiger when we were at the doctor's office, or at the hospital, for that matter?" I asked. While I'd love to believe that, there were just too many holes in the theory. "I think it has to do with getting angry and my not being able to switch back was just a lucky coincidence."

"You only transitioned back when there was no more danger."

"I'm aware of that," I snapped and rolled out of bed. "I need some clothes," I said with my back to him. The bed creaked and a moment later, he wrapped a bathrobe around my shoulders.

"This is all that's down here," he said, crossing into my field of vision and tying the sash to his bathrobe. "Everything else is upstairs and, based on what happened today, I think we should get the hell out of here as soon as possible. I already moved the car. It's in the garage here for now and I didn't lock the workshop, so anyone can get in."

"What about the hatch?"

"The truck is sitting over it and surrounded by boxes. I still need to weld it shut along with the door at the end of the tunnel. But that should take less than an hour. Then we should bolt."

I wasn't ready to leave yet, but we really had no choice, not when Lucifer's hellhounds found us so easily. It stood to reason that he'd soon follow and we didn't want to be anywhere near here when he arrived.

"What about Ted and Valerie?"

"She isn't out of danger and he doesn't have any idea when she'll be ready to be released," Damian said. "And I told Ted to find somewhere else to stay until she was good to come home."

"We might have a problem," I said, shifting and meeting his gaze.

He tensed and crossed his arms. "What?"

"The ex-FBI agent lives in York."

Damian's expression hardened, but before he could balk, I added, "He's the only one on the news who didn't jump to the conclusion that you killed those people. He said he spoke to a witness, a cafeteria worker who saw what happened. He said you weren't responsible for the officer's death, despite the evidence stacked against you. The cops disagree. Considering the surveillance video, they severed the agent's connection to the case. That's when I got pissed. Lucifer is doing a hell of a job setting you up."

"I'm aware of what that bastard is doing, and now we have a garage smeared with blood. I'd bet my left arm there will be a missing person reported and he'll make sure the blood in the garage is matched to the victim."

"But the dogs?"

Damian pointed toward the tunnel. "You missed the coup d'état. The hellhounds disintegrated, so it's just a bloody mess."

"Jesus," I whispered, my mind turning this additional fact over. It was like Lucifer intentionally sent those beasts into the slaughterhouse. "It would have been better if the carcasses were found, even though they would have been a real bizarre find."

Damian sent a sarcastic smile. "That would have made things eons better," he said and ran his hand through his tussled hair. "Should we change our plans and head to Greece?"

I blew a stream of air from my lips, considering his offer, but I knew damn well both cops and Lucifer's henchmen would pack the airports. "No. I think we need to look up that agent. He's the only one who believed you weren't responsible, and both the cops and reporters made him look like a fool."

"He'd hand us over in a heartbeat," Damian said.

"Well, if he tries, I can always turn tiger," I said and forced a smile, but the prospect of hurting a human made me feel sick to my stomach. I swallowed the burn in the back of my throat. "But I don't think he will. Before he got into his car, he said if we wanted someone on our side, to look him up."

Damian rolled his eyes. "It's a bullshit ploy," he said, raising my irritation level.

"I know bullshit when I see it," I said. "This wasn't. Besides, I'd rather take my chances with him than the cops, because you know damn well if we end up in a jail cell, neither one of us will walk out alive." The memory of the roadblock in New York City crossed my mind. The sheer number of police officers Lucifer commanded had chilled my blood, and even the memory made me shiver.

"How do you know this guy isn't in Lucifer's pocket?" Damian asked as if he had got a whiff of my memory.

I focused on him. "I don't."

"Then why the hell do we even chance it?"

We stared at each other, and I sighed. "It's just one of those things, Damian. I trusted him. I don't know how to explain it better than that."

"What's his name?"

"Special Agent Steve Williams."

"As soon as I finish welding the doors, I'll find his address. While I'm doing that, do you mind packing things upstairs?"

I didn't mind, especially with him safeguarding the house from demons and other preternatural creatures. My gaze dropped to his leg. "Do you have any bandages down here?" I pointed to his still oozing wound.

"I don't think so," he said and turned, disappearing into the bathroom. The creak of a door drifted on the quiet, followed by the crinkle of a package being opened. When he stepped out, a six-inch bandage covered the cut. "I guess Michael stocked us up," he added and pressed his lips together.

Damian's hands found his waist, and his head dropped to his chest. It wasn't until I saw the shake of his shoulders that I realized he was crying. I crossed and lifted his chin. His crystal-blue eyes swam with tears and more clear drops traced lines on his face.

"I guess grief hits at the damnedest times," he said and laughed, swiping the tears from his face like they were an unforgiveable offense.

My heart squeezed in my chest and I wrapped my arms around him. He returned the hug for a minute and then planted a kiss on my cheek.

"I don't have time for this right now," he mumbled and stepped away, heading back into the bathroom. This time, when he came out, he wore the clothes he had on when we were attacked and I started to speak, but he held up his hand.

"I'll change after I'm done." He pointed toward the tunnel and then stepped out of the bedroom, leaving me with my own sense of loss.

Trinity Rising
Chapter Ten
Naomi

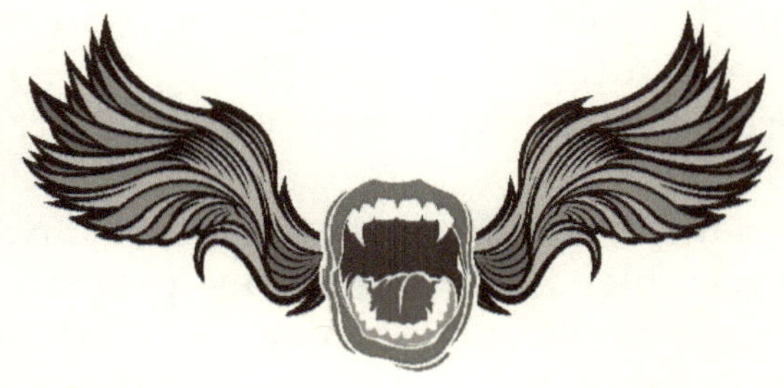

I DROPED THE DUFFEL bags into the trunk of the Aston Martin and retreated to the living room, irritated that the only comfortable thing I found to wear was a pair of Damian's sweat pants. My cell buzzed, and I picked it up from the table, glancing at the caller ID. It wasn't Valerie, so I answered the call.

"Hello?"

"Hello, Mrs. Andreas?"

"Yes," I said, trying to place the vaguely familiar voice.

He cleared his throat. "Mrs. Andreas, this is Dr. Wolk," he said and his tone set off a wealth of alarms through my form, jolting my heart into a pounding rhythm and my grip on my phone tightened.

I swallowed the dry fear from my mouth. "What can I do for you?"

"Well, there seems to be an issue with your blood sample."

"Diabetes?"

"No, at least not in this sample. It looks like someone introduced feline DNA with yours. I'm sorry for the mixup, but we need you to come back in for another blood test."

I stared out the window. "What do you mean feline DNA?"

"The sample had a trace of feline DNA along with yours, like a cat hair was present in the vial, so all we can surmise is that the lab screwed up or the containers were contaminated."

I sat down heavily on the couch. "Um, we're headed out of the country to visit Damian's relatives. Can I follow up with you when we get back?"

There was silence on the line and then a hurried, "That will be fine, thank you for understanding." A dial tone stretched through the line and I disconnected the call.

I was still in shock when Damian stepped into the room with a box in his arms. He put it on the table and met my gaze.

"What's up?"

I stared at the computer and peripherals sticking out of the box and then looked up at him. "I don't have diabetes, but apparently my blood contains traces of feline DNA."

His eyebrows arched and he slid onto the couch.

"They think it's a lab error, or a contaminated vial, but..." I trailed off. I thought the tiger was a left over result of the shadow virus. Damian sat with his mouth open in shock, so he obviously thought the same thing. He blinked and cocked his head.

"Does that mean my blood contains traces of hawk DNA?"

I didn't even want to consider the ramifications of what this meant for the baby in my belly, but one image kept flashing before my eyes. The symbol for my grandfather's specific bloodline: a winged-tiger.

"They wanted me to come down for another blood test, but I told him we were headed out of the country."

"Quick thinking," Damian said and stood, retreating to the bedroom to change. He hadn't said a word about my attire, and I appreciated it. He returned in the clean clothing I had laid out for him and dropped his dirty clothing in the garbage, sealing it and dumping it out in the garage.

"You about ready?" he asked after he finished packing his laptop and note pads that were scattered over the coffee table.

I looked up at him, still in shock from the news. "You did everything, including fixing the keypad?"

He nodded. "It took a little longer than I wanted though," he said and I glanced at the clock.

A little over an hour had passed since I started packing. Of course, it took me forever to find something that fit over my belly. "We might need to go shopping before we find a place to stay," I said and stood, waving toward the sweats. "I had nothing that fit."

He pressed his lips into a tight smile. His attempt at hiding the budding humor lost, and instead of addressing the breach in manners, he picked up the box and disappeared into the garage.

"Did you want to do a quick walk through?" he asked, and I nodded.

"I already packed the mural," I said. That was the one thing that followed us from place to place, and I know it meant a great deal to him. He gave a nod and pulled out his phone. I turned away, heading to the bedroom and scanning the vacant dresser shelves. Opening and closing drawers and dressers before doing the same in the bathroom. On impulse, I grabbed the first aid kit and opened it, dumping the headache remedies, anti-biotic ointment and bandages into the box before clipping it closed.

Damian held my coat open as I stepped into the living room. He had Ted's thick hunting jacket on instead of the sleek leather he usually wore.

"I figured Ted could use something fancier than this. Especially since this one is better for packing," he said. "I also have all the extra ammunition for his nine-millimeter stored in the trunk."

"Does he know?" I said, feeling the first bite of irritation, but it disappeared with a nod from Damian.

"He doesn't know I left him my coat, but I asked if we could take the gun. He has no issue with it and in a few weeks, he'll report it stolen. In the meantime, he'll keep us informed of

Valerie's condition," he said and led me to the car.

"Ready?" he asked once he settled into the driver's seat.

"I'm ready. Are you?" I asked, glancing at his shaking hands.

He followed my gaze and chuckled. "I have to admit, I'm a little nervous. I don't know what's waiting for us out there."

Trinity Rising
Chapter Eleven
Damian

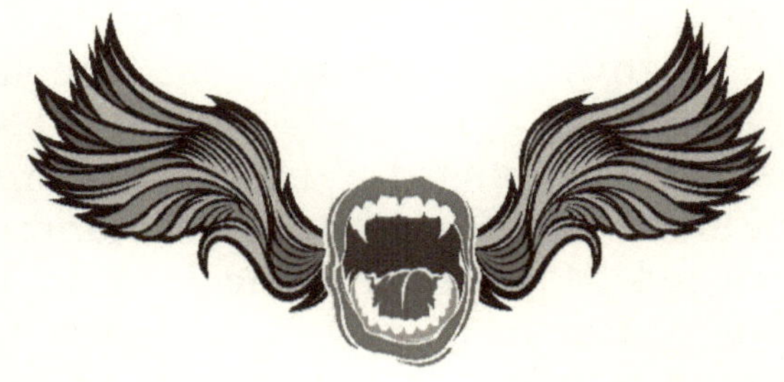

EVERY MUSCLE IN MY body tensed as we pulled out of the garage. I waited until the door had closed before turning the car around in the driveway. I gave Naomi a cursory glance and took a deep breath, pressing the gate controls as I approached.

No one was visible in the vicinity and after pulling through the gate, I pushed the button, waiting until the gate clicked closed, then I gunned it, turning toward the nearest highway route. I kept glancing in my rearview, expecting a tail, but there was nothing on the road behind us, or in front of us, for that matter, and I gave a relieved laugh as the house disappeared from view.

"Knock on wood," I said and gave Naomi's hand a squeeze. She responded with only a strained smile before she continued her darting scan of the landscape.

"I don't think..."

"Shush. Not until we are a safe distance away, okay?"

I nodded consent and focused on the road. The only cars that pulled out behind us turned down different roads and by the time we pulled onto the highway, I relaxed enough to fully exhale.

When we passed the Welcome to Massachusetts sign, I glanced at Naomi again and shrugged. "I guess my checking in for our flight out of Hartford may have given us just enough of a window to get out of there." The muscles in my shoulders relaxed a notch.

"When did you do that?"

"Right before I reprogrammed the basement keypad." I glanced at the clock on the display. "The plane will start boarding in another half hour. Just long enough for us to put a little more distance between us and the airport."

"He's not going to buy that we went to Michigan with the cars?" she asked.

"No, not with us killing his dogs. I have a feeling they were sent on a suicide mission just to prove we were still there." I finally voiced my thoughts and the wound on my leg flared, sending an itch that made my hands grip the wheel tighter.

"I've been meaning to ask. Hellhounds talk?"

Her question made me raise an eyebrow in her direction. "What?"

"When you asked the hellhound what he wanted, he spoke."

I couldn't help the laugh. "No, baby, it just growled up a fucking storm."

She laughed as well, but something about the tone of it pulled my gaze to hers. "Actually, they were sent to bring your head back. At least that's the answer I heard."

The shock of her words left me quiet and I glance at her, wondering just what kind of freak she was. The worry in her eyes calmed me. If she was a freak, it didn't matter. She's the one that saved my sorry ass. Again.

"My head, huh?" I asked, and she nodded. "I can see that," I replied and took her hand, bringing it to my lips. "If you hadn't come, I'd be dog chow by now."

"You were doing a pretty good job with the crowbar."

I chuckled. "If you say so." Whether she admitted it, I knew I wouldn't have survived and the garage floor would have been stained with my flesh and blood. I shivered at the thought.

The traffic was pretty light, and we pulled off the highway exactly three hours later and I pulled into the first gas station off the exit ramp and parked by the pumps. Naomi scuttled out of the car towards the building, walking fast with her thighs together, and I grinned. The car still idled, and I turned the ignition key, shutting off the engine and stretched before I reached down and popped the gas cap. As I pulled my wallet out, I paused, wondering if using a credit card would alert Lucifer to our whereabouts.

"Shit," I mumbled and opted for cash, pulling a twenty out of the billfold and heading inside to pre-pay. While I was inside, I grabbed a couple of bottles of water and stepped to the counter as the bathroom door opened and Naomi came out.

She grabbed a candy bar and some mints and added them to my tab.

I paid just as the door jingled and as I turned; I handed Naomi the bag with the drinks. She took it and looked up at the man in the doorway, freezing on the spot. Her widening eyes made me look closer at the stranger.

The man stared at me, just as wide-eyed as Naomi.

"Oh, hey, Agent Williams, how are you?" the kid behind the counter asked, and the man sent a nod in his direction.

"I'm good, John. Didn't you need to check something in the stockroom?" he said and a cold shiver traversed my spine as the kid nodded and disappeared into the back of the store, leaving the three of us alone.

A base warning in the pit of my stomach said to run, to get away as soon as possible, and my heart clenched in my chest. I reached into my jacket, wrapping my hand around the handle of my revolver, but the flutter of wings caught me off guard and I stepped back, my eyes darting around to find the source.

"Be careful, Steve," the voice whispered, and Naomi stepped back as well, her hand shooting out to grab my elbow.

When my gaze landed on Agent Williams, he was assessing me with narrowed eyes.

"Why don't you give me the gun, son," he said and put out his hand.

I blinked as I pulled the gun out of my pocket, almost as if I had no control, but instead of handing it over, I pointed it at him.

"Damian," Naomi gasped.

"I don't want any trouble," I said, and the agent cocked his head, looking between the gun and me as if perplexed.

"Give me the gun," he said more forcefully, and I felt a tickle in my mind, followed by the instinct to give him our only weapon.

"I don't think so," I said, resisting the urge, and another flutter caught my attention. "Why are you following us?" I asked. That was the only justification I had for him being here at the same time. After all, he was a cop.

He let out a quick laugh. "I wasn't following you. This is completely coincidence and from the look on your faces, you know exactly who I am."

"And you know who I am."

He nodded. "Yes. I suggest you put the gun away before someone else comes in or John figures out he really didn't need anything from the back room." He glanced up at the camera in the corner and then back at me. "If you're not going to give it to me, put the damn thing away."

I laughed. "Why? So you can arrest us?"

The tension in the room mounted and wings fluttered yet again, along with another warning directly to Agent Williams.

"What's with the angel?" Naomi spouted, and both our gazes dropped to hers. She wasn't looking directly at Steve. Instead, her gaze was over his shoulder to the right, as if a ghost I couldn't see stood at his side.

"You can see him?" Steve said, pulling my attention back to him. He looked just as shocked as I felt.

"Sort of, but he doesn't seem to be a dick like Lu..." She stopped and covered her mouth before she conjured the bastard by mistake.

"We have to go," I said and stowed the gun in my pocket. The proximity of any angel to where we were only meant trouble, and I wasn't sticking around to find out whether this man was on our side or not.

"I'm on your side," Agent Williams said and planted his feet, blocking the only exit.

"Bullshit. You're a cop."

"Ex-cop," he said. "And why would being close to an angel be an issue for you?"

A jolt zapped me, creating a prickly tickle all over my skin, and I stared at him. "You... can read minds?"

The cocky smile and nod confirmed it. "I can do a hell of a lot more than that," he said. "Gas up your car and follow me. I need some answers."

I straightened my back. "While that sounds charming, I think I'll pass," I said. "Besides, I don't give a shit what you need. We're out of here." I glanced at Naomi. "This was a bad idea," I said and started for the door. If he didn't get out of my way, I'd run him over and his gaze narrowed, reading my intentions correctly.

"I can be your best friend or your worst fucking nightmare. It's your choice, kid."

I ignored him, but Naomi pulled back on my arm. I peeled her hand off, meeting her frightened gaze. "I'll be fine," I whispered and turned back to Agent Williams.

"I don't think you want to do that," he warned as I approached and I let out a strained laugh as every muscle in my body tightened, ready for battle.

He didn't yield, instead he stood his ground, his hands curling into fists as well and when he shifted into a ready stance, I stopped, recognizing the form.

"Karate?"

He just nodded, and for a brief instant, I thought it might be nice to spar again. I hadn't truly sparred in years.

Agent Williams raised an eyebrow. "Years? What were you, a toddler?"

It was my turn to send a sarcastic smile. "I'm a master in a few different schools," I said, prompting a laugh from him as he sized me up.

"You aren't old enough," he said with authority.

I glanced at Naomi and then back at him. I'm sure my life story would completely blow his mind, but I kept a wrap on my thoughts.

"Please move, Agent Williams," I said. "I need to fill my car."

He shook his head, and I stepped in, throwing the first punch. When his hand closed around my fist, stopping it from connecting, the world swam in front of my eyes and I wasn't the only one who gasped. Like a hyped up download, the man's entire life flashed like a bizarre slide show in my head.

Everything he experienced right up to this moment downloaded into my brain and I inhaled, yanking away as if contact with his skin had produced burning blisters.

His face remained pale and his jaw slack as he stared at me. It took me a moment to understand the transference that occurred.

If I saw his entire life...

"What just happened?" Naomi whispered, and I turned to her.

"Nothing," I said, and we walked past the stunned agent to the car. I helped her into the front seat and pumped the pre-paid amount into my car. I kept glancing at the store, expecting Agent Williams to come out, but he hadn't recovered from the glimpse of my life he received.

Hell, I couldn't blame him. His life was bizarre enough, but the existence of vampires alone must have blown his logical circuitry right out of the water. When I finished, I returned the pump to the holder and closed the gas cap.

Agent Williams still hadn't come out, and I sighed as I slipped into the driver's seat, waiting for him to get his bearings.

"Where are we going?" Naomi asked.

"To his house," I said and nodded toward the store. Agent Williams finally stepped outside, still looking like he had seen a thousand ghosts.

Naomi looked at him and then back at me. "What happened in there?"

I gave her a laugh. "Special Agent Williams isn't normal by any means," I said, and her head snapped to him.

"What is he?"

"Oh, he's human, but he's supercharged." She turned back to me and her brow creased. "Did you ever watch Star Trek?" I asked, and her brow creased even more. "The only description I can think of is he did a Vulcan mind meld on me."

The crease in her brow altered into the incredulous arches. "What?"

"I saw his life and by the look on his face, he saw mine."

Her head snapped in his direction as Agent Williams slipped into his car. His hands visibly shook, and I started laughing, prompting Naomi to bring her gaze back to me.

"What do you mean by supercharged?"

I sighed and started the car, pulling out behind the vintage BMW. "His psychic powers are beyond anything I have ever encountered in a human." I was still digesting all I saw and his life was full of some of the same challenges and devastations as mine. "But you were right. He is on our side." I glanced at her. "And it's a damned good thing."

Trinity Rising
Chapter Twelve
Damian

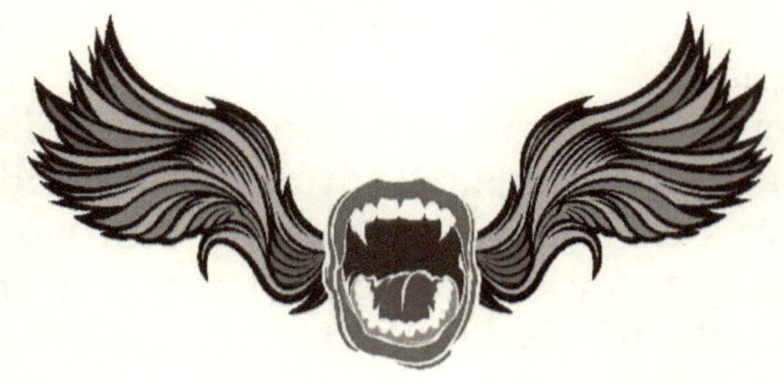

WE DROVE IN SILENCE and by the time we pulled up to the gate surrounding his house, I'd had time to think about our predicament and wondered if this was really a good thing or not. If Lucifer got wind of this man and all his talents, we might end up as a secondary trophy.

I hesitated before following him inside and when I parked in the driveway behind him; I glanced at the gate closing behind us. He got out of his car and just stared at me. After a moment, he shook his head like clearing thoughts and the glare he leveled at me made me second-guess this.

I stepped out of the car and circled around to Naomi, helping her out.

Agent Williams waited in the garage and I approached him.

"What kind of fool do you think I am?" he snarled when I got within the confines of the garage.

"Denial? That's what you're going with?" I huffed. That should have been what I expected based on the man's history, but it still caught me off guard.

His eyes narrowed, and he crossed his arms. The garage door engaged, dropping behind us.

"There's no fucking way what I saw was real."

I thought for a moment, scanning through the contents of his life. "Your life hasn't been a walk in the park, either."

Naomi shifted, and she cleared her throat.

"Can I use your bathroom?" she asked with a small voice that cut through the tension. His gaze dropped to her.

"I'm supposed to believe you..." he waved at her and blinked, his gaze dropping to her belly. He nodded instead and turned, leading us into the family room of his home. "The bathroom is down there." He pointed to a small hallway on the other side of the kitchen.

He waited until she was out of sight and turned to me.

"I'm not sure what to call you, considering," I said. "Special Agent Williams seems a bit formal, don't you think?"

"That shit can't be real," he said and crossed his arms.

"If you don't believe what you saw, have your angel friend ask Michael directly."

Wings fluttered, and the winged man in Agent William's memory appeared for a moment. "I can't. I'm not allowed in heaven. At least, not yet," he said.

I studied him, watching as he faded to nothing, and finally I shook my head, refocusing on Agent Williams. His relationship with his guardian angel was as bizarre as some things in my life and as I focused on those memories, a flood of secondary memories filtered up from a lower level and I raised an eyebrow.

"So you're telling me you're twenty-five hundred years old?"

I nodded, and he sat down on the couch.

"And there are such things as vampires?" he asked, pinching the bridge of his nose.

"Well, there were. I think Eve was the last one."

"And Lu..." he started and pressed his lips closed along with his eyes. "And archangels, fallen or otherwise, exist?"

"Yes."

"And your wife can transform into a white tiger?" He opened his eyes, his voice carrying the incredulous spin of someone whose world was crumbling around them.

I smiled and shrugged. "You forgot demons," I added.

"I already believed in demons." A shadow passed over his face.

The memory filtered up to the forefront of my mind, and I gave him a quick nod. He just stared at me in silent awe that made me uncomfortable. I shifted, unsure of whether I should sit.

"Well, doesn't that just beat all?" He ran both hands through his hair. "So, what I saw in that poor cafeteria worker's mind really happened?"

"Yes. The devil slayed Michael and ate his heart."

Naomi shuffled back into the room with pale cheeks and wet eyelashes. She blinked and gave me that sickly smile. From the looks of it, her morning sickness was acting up again.

"Agent Williams, you wouldn't happen to have any ginger-ale?" I asked.

He stood and crossed to the refrigerator, pulling out a can and handed it to Naomi and then turned back to me. "Call me Steve," he said. "Can I get you a drink?"

I smiled and stuffed my hands into my pocket. "Scotch," I said, knowing that was his drink of choice as well.

He brought two glasses and set them on the coffee table and retrieved a bottle of Glendronach. I nodded my approval, and he poured me a glass.

"It may take me a little while to digest all that I've seen. In the meantime, you might want to do that angel proofing thing." He raised his glass.

"Do you have a bar of soap?"

"I think we have one in the bathroom cabinet." He pointed the same way Naomi came. "Why?"

"I know it works on archangels, but I have no idea if it will trap him here, so I figured you probably don't want the symbols to be permanent."

"I don't know about that," he said and gulped his drink down.

"Fuck you, Williams," the voice spat out, and I couldn't help but smile. His relationship with his guardian angel was one I didn't quite understand, even with the history I received.

"You seem to be a magnet for redeemed killers," I said and received a snort from the air, followed by laughter. Instead of continuing the conversation, I turned in search of soap because, between the three of us, someone was bound to fuck up and say Lucifer's name out loud.

I drew the symbols on all the first-floor windows as low in the corner as possible, trying to make them inconspicuous. I drew it on the front door, garage door and the back sliders as well. Any place that allowed passage between the inside and outside was marked. When I finished, I stepped back into the family room and pointed to the ceiling.

"Yeah, go ahead," Steve nodded and continued his conversation with Naomi.

I took my time; not only drawing the angel hex, but also digesting the memories I had been given. When I completed my rounds, I dropped the soap in the soap dish in the upstairs bathroom, cleaning off my fingertips before returning downstairs.

"When do you think your family will return?" I asked, rounding the last step.

Steve looked at the clock and then at me. "Anytime."

I nodded and slid next to Naomi. "How are you feeling?" I asked and rubbed her belly.

"Okay," she said, and I knew she was lying. Her cheeks were too pale and dark rings appeared under her eyes.

"Did you need to lie down?" Steve asked, and Naomi hesitated.

"We're safe for the moment," I said and moved my gaze to Steve's. "Right?"

He nodded. "We have a couple of guest rooms," he said and stood. "Let me show you where they are. I'm also assuming that you two will be our guests tonight?" he asked, glancing at me.

"Honestly, I hadn't thought that far in advance." I met Naomi's gaze, and she shrugged, leaving the decision to me. She was too tired to function right now and needed sleep. "We'll play it by ear," I replied.

"When my wife was pregnant, she used to shut down all of a sudden, too," I heard Steve say as he escorted her upstairs.

Left to my own devices, I poured another glass of scotch and stepped to the sliding glass doors leading to their backyard. A covered pool took up half of the vast lawn and the ocean view was stellar. I had to give it to Naomi. This place was beautiful. Colder than Greece, but it would do.

The sound of the garage opening pulled my attention to the door we entered and the man who stepped in the house a few minutes later could have passed as my twin. I shuffled through Steve's memories and readily identified him as CJ Ryan.

He blinked and stopped, blocking the doorway as he stared at me with wide eyes.

"Who are you?" he asked and stepped aside, letting the rest of the family into the house.

"Damian Andreas," I said and turned to face them, their names coming just as quickly as their faces appeared. Tom Ryan and his wife Raven followed by Steve's wife, Jennifer.

Raven nearly dropped her bags when her gaze fell on me, and what color had been in her face bled out. The way CJ's gaze shot to her, and then back to me, made me shift. For a moment, I wished for Naomi in tiger form standing next to me. With her formidable force, I'd feel a hell of a lot safer than I did right now.

CJ's eyes narrowed, and he crossed, dumping his bag on the table. I knew enough about him to feel the discomfort prickle through me when he turned a glare in my direction. An unfamiliar tingle encompassed my head, and I realized he was trying to force his way into my mind.

"Your father was nice enough to show my wife to a bedroom upstairs. He should be down in a minute," I said, doing my best to block his probe.

The creak of the stairs pulled my gaze away and Steve appeared.

"I see you've met my family," he said.

"Yes. Is Naomi okay?" I asked and took a sip of the scotch, irritated with the slight shake in my hand that knocked the ice cubes against the glass.

"I think she was out the moment her head hit the pillow. Reminds me of Jen when she was pregnant," Steve said.

He met my gaze, and I swear I saw a flash of sorrow cross his features. After all the years, losing his children still created a visual pain. I doubted my ability to carry on if I lost my children, and they hadn't even been born yet, so the fact that Steve had been able to function at all increased my admiration.

Steve turned to his wife. "They're going to be staying with us for a while," he said.

"Just tonight," I corrected, and an awkward silence filled the room. The rest of Steve's family just stared at me and Raven blanched a little more, shifting, so her husband buffered her from view.

"What is he?" Raven whispered to CJ, thinking she spoke softly enough, but I caught it and glanced at her, trying to stifle a laugh.

"I'm sorry for laughing, Raven, but there really is no straightforward answer to that question." Everyone's eyes widened and their gazes traveled to Steve.

He shrugged. "We had a transfer of sorts," he said.

"Isn't he the one who killed those cops in Connecticut?" CJ asked, pointing in my direction.

"No." Steve stepped into the room and crossed to the table, picking up his glass. "He's being set up."

CJ stared at him, then he wobbled, reaching for the table and sitting in the nearest chair, his eyes widening in shock, and then his gaze traveled to me. "I think maybe you guys should unpack the groceries and go get dinner somewhere."

"Why?" Tom asked, his gaze bouncing between Steve, Raven and CJ before meeting mine, and then they traveled to the fluttering wings next to Steve.

"Steve?" Jennifer asked.

He glanced at me, and I sighed.

"I'm putting you at risk," I said. "They have a right to know what could be coming."

Tom's hands flew in a pattern I didn't recognize, but the question in his gaze was enough.

CJ hadn't stopped staring at me, and even his complexion blanched.

"What might be coming?" Jennifer asked.

"Armageddon," CJ answered, and a silent chill blanketed the room.

Trinity Rising
Chapter Thirteen
Damian

"YOU KNOW I HAVE an open mind, especially with what happened to us in college," Jennifer said as she sat down next to Steve on the couch. "But this. This is way too out there for me to even comprehend."

I had been talking for a couple of hours, trying to recap my life and our plight. The groceries had long been put away, five large pizza boxes sat on the kitchen table picked over, and the remaining half dozen pieces on a plate set aside for Naomi.

Tom and Raven kept their distance, giving me the greatest berth, because even though the others had warmed up to my being in their home, Raven still couldn't look at me and when she did her expression was tense, like I was going to self-destruct at any moment and I focused on her for a minute.

"May I ask you a question?" I asked before her gaze flitted away again.

She pointed at her chest, and I nodded. "I... I guess," she answered.

"What are you seeing that everyone else can't?" I had enough history from Steve to know she saw auras, but she hadn't been able to look at me more than a cursory glance since she came in.

"You're too bright for me to look at for any length of time. It's like looking into the sun," she said. "And if I squint, I can see a shadow of... of wings mingled with it." She squinted and then blinked away. "But it's not like CJ's father's wings, not angel wings."

"When I was a vampire, I could change into a hawk at will," I said, and everyone's gaze jumped back to me. I hadn't included my ability to transition into a wild bird in my conversation, but I had explained the shadow virus and our near demise at Lucifer's hands. They also knew his plans if he ever got a hold of Naomi. "Something about the combination of shadow virus and angel blood."

"I turn into a tiger," Naomi's voice broke everyone's stare, and the relief I had at the sight of her rumpled hair and sleepy eyes was more than in my mind. The knot I developed in the middle of my back loosened and I stood. "Naomi, this is Steve's wife, Jennifer," I started introductions. "And this is Tom and his wife, Raven."

"Nice to meet you," she said and received nods in response. Raven's squint was less pronounced when she viewed Naomi, but it was there.

"She has the same aura?" I asked and Raven glanced in my general direction, but her gaze was averted toward the ground.

"No. It reminds me a little of CJ's aura."

I caught Naomi's gaze. "Michael's grace," we both said at the same time. That was the only logical explanation I could conceive. The grace of an archangel must be glaring.

CJ turned and stood. "I'm CJ," he said, finishing the introductions.

Naomi's eyes widened, flashing between my doppelganger and me. She let out a nervous laugh. "You two could be twins," she said.

A moment passed where their eyes locked, and then he offered her his seat. The blatant interest painted on his face sent a burning irritation through my core, landing in my stomach and churning like a time bomb. He glanced at me and raised an eyebrow and for the first time in over a millennium, I tasted the bitter pill of jealousy.

He returned his gaze to Naomi. "Can I get you some pizza?" he asked and Naomi nodded, still staring at him in a way that burned my insides.

Silence blanketed the room, and Steve's brow creased as he glanced at me. A smirk appeared on his face and he slid his glance to his wife, sharing a silent communication that I was not privy to. By the sudden appearance and suppression of a smile, I guessed he was broadcasting my discomfort with their son's chivalrous behavior.

Naomi's gaze followed him and I set my drink on the table and stood.

"I need some air," I said and turned without explaining. The chill slapped at me as I stepped out of the sliding glass doors into the backyard. The cold Atlantic beckoned in the distance and I crossed the expanse of yard to a quaint rock wall that separated the yard from a fifteen-foot drop into the ocean.

I shoved my hands into my pockets and scanned the vastness before me.

A few minutes passed and despite the frigid breeze, I remained in my spot, trying to isolate why I was suddenly feeling so insecure about Naomi. She was bound to me by marriage and blood, and yet, I was afraid that she'd run to the nearest man with an honest and pure heart.

"You really have nothing to worry about," CJ said, stepping next to me. "Your wife loves you."

I glanced at him and then back at the water. "I know she does, but I've never had any competition before," I admitted, knowing he was privy to my train of thought.

He chuckled in a way that pulled my attention to him.

"I didn't think it was a competition," he said.

"So you're not interested in Naomi," I stated, hoping to put my mind at ease. I glanced back at the sunset painting the clouds, turning everything the purple-pink of twilight.

Silence drifted between us, and I turned toward him, meeting his gaze.

"No comment?" I asked, and he gave me the kind of smile that I always equated with Lucifer; cocky and certain that he held the winning hand. I clenched my teeth, sending a glare at him.

"Look, if this was a competition, you would lose. But it isn't, so just fucking relax, will ya?"

"I wouldn't lose." I crossed my arms and scanned the sea once more before trudging back into the warm house. Naomi looked up from the kitchen table where Jennifer sat with her. She tilted her head, questioning me without words, and I shrugged. She didn't need to know just how unhinged I was right now.

"Where'd everyone go?" I asked, sliding into the seat next to her.

"Steve went to change and Tom and Raven decided to catch a movie in Portsmouth," Jennifer said and we all glanced as CJ stepped inside and took a seat on the couch. "Are you really as old as Steve says?"

"I'm twenty-five," I said. "Of course, I've been twenty-five for over two thousand years, but who's counting?"

She glanced at Naomi for confirmation and got a nod in return. When her gaze landed back on me, she asked, "Did you have a chance to meet Jesus?"

I laughed. "I've met many people, ma'am, and yes; the messiah was one of them."

"What was he like?"

"Interesting. He had a lot of good ideas, and an honest heart. Of course, I had already been introduced to Michael and angel bloodlines, so the idea of God's child wasn't as farfetched as some people thought." I glanced at Naomi. "I can tell you this much though, he has got to be livid that so many acts of violence have been perpetrated in his name. He was a peaceful man, but had no tolerance for those who skewed the word of the Lord for their own gain."

Jennifer looked down at her hands. "And heaven?"

When her gaze returned to mine, I knew where she was going with the questions. Even with the existence of a guardian angel looking over her husband, she still had doubts and worries about where her children's souls were. I sent her a soft smile and a nod. "Yes. There's a heaven," I said, and the relief swept over her face. "And I'm sure your daughters are there."

Jennifer blinked her tears back and gave me a quick nod.

Naomi watched the exchange, her brow furrowing with questions, and I shook my head. She let it go and focused back on the conversation, but I could tell she understood. She blinked, studying the woman at the table with the same admiration as I felt for both Jennifer and Steve.

"What was your favorite era?" Jennifer asked.

My gaze moved to Naomi. "Right now," I said, with no hesitation.

A snort from the couch pulled my attention and CJ sent a glance over his shoulder, his derision snaking over me like a hangman's noose.

I knew it was poor manners, but I shot the question out, anyway. "What the hell is your issue?"

CJ stood, turning toward me. "You. You're my issue," he pointed at me. "They think you're something special, but all I see is someone who killed for sport, like my father did. But in this case, you did it for centuries upon centuries."

"Damian didn't kill for sport," Naomi said before I could form a response.

CJ challenged her with an arch of his eyebrow.

"He's right," I said, pulling her gaze to mine. "I killed with abandon, but I only killed those worthy of death. So, in that way, I differ from your father."

"Who are you to judge?" CJ said.

I stood, crossing the distance, extending my hand.

"Go ahead," I challenged, knowing he had the same power to siphon memories as Steve.

He looked at my hand, and the muscles in his jaw jumped. When his gaze locked on mine, he reached out. The moment our skin contacted, a rush of memories assaulted me. Sound swirled around me and a power I couldn't comprehend gripped every muscle. CJ's memories flooded my mind, just like Steve's had, but there was something else that came with them that hadn't been transferred when Steve did his mind meld.

Just before his grip loosened, I felt the power crawling back into its host and the room came into clear view. In my mind's eye, I reached out, grabbing hold of the last ribbon of magic, feeling a piece tear off and settle inside me.

CJ's gaze hardened, and he yanked his hand from my grip. He stepped back, rubbing his palm, just staring at me. He looked down at his hand and back, like I was still the shadow being, his silence just as unnerving as the flurry of memories.

Whispers, like faint echoes, caressed my ears, but I kept my gaze on CJ, waiting for his judgment. Instead of speaking, he slowly lowered to the couch.

He licked his lips, formulating broken thoughts before speaking.

"You really are an angel's descendent." It wasn't a question, just a statement that I let hang on the air for a full beat.

"Do you think I'd really spend the last few hours bullshitting you?"

"Actually, that's exactly what I thought. I couldn't read much from either of you." He glanced between Naomi and I. "I just thought you were here to pull one over on us and you somehow snowed Uncle Steve. I couldn't figure out what your deal was."

"And now?"

"At least I know you're not a liar," he said.

Trinity Rising
Chapter Fourteen
Damian

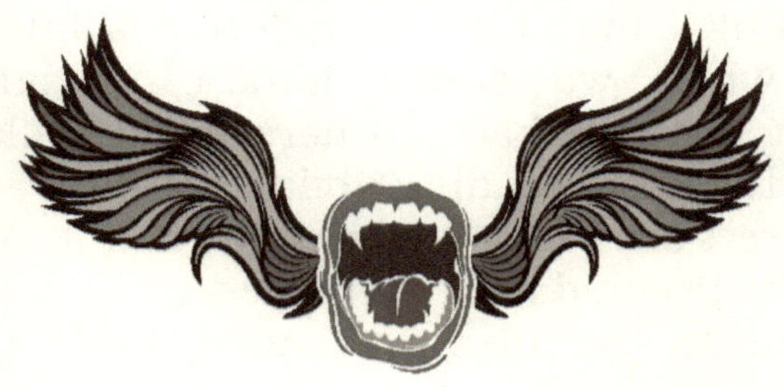

NAOMI OFFERED ME A tired smile as I sat down on the edge of the bed.

"I'm not tired," I said and brushed the hair from her face before planting a soft kiss on her lips. The whispers continued, and I shook my head, wondering just what the hell I was hearing. "Do you hear anything funny?"

She shook her head. "Why?"

"Because I feel like I'm in a theater and everyone is whispering."

Naomi let out a little laugh and I could have sworn she said, *you're so weird sometimes*, but her lips never moved. Still, it was her voice in my head, and I studied her.

"I'm not weird," I said, testing the waters, and her eyes widened.

Holy shit, you can hear me?

I started laughing. It had been a couple of months since I could hear her in my head and I missed being able to read her. On the heels of realizing I could hear her thoughts; I realized the buzz I was hearing were the random thoughts of the others in the household. My smile faded, and I glanced at the door.

"I think I may have transferred a bit of CJ's talent when we shook hands," I said and brought my gaze back to hers. If I'd pulled in a little of his mind reading ability...

Before I could complete the thought, a knock on the bedroom door interrupted us.

"Come in," I called and stood, half-expecting CJ.

When Steve pushed open the door, I met his stare.

"We need to talk," he said.

I nodded and turned to Naomi. "I'll be up in a while," I said and headed out of the room, meeting his gaze as I closed the door.

"CJ thinks you may have gotten some of his shine."

"That's what you're calling it?" I asked, avoiding the question.

"Stop being such a cocky son of a bitch." He turned, expecting me to follow. He stopped at the top of the stairs, and I got a hint of frustration. He wasn't able to read me or command me like a normal human. Transferring memories had been incidental, something he hadn't intended, especially after ordering me to give him my gun, and I didn't comply.

Now he was even more wary of me and instead of pushing his buttons and taking advantage of his hostility, I followed him downstairs, where CJ sat flipping through the television channels.

He tossed the remote onto the table and glared at me.

I didn't give you permission to take any of my juice, he thought, and I shrugged.

"Look, I didn't plan on it either," I said, taking the seat on the opposite couch.

"How did you do that?" Steve asked.

"Honestly, I'm not sure. I felt the infusion of power when we shook hands and when it retreated, I guess I grabbed onto a piece."

They exchanged a glance, and I took a minute to study their histories. Steve had done something similar, but in his case, it was the full absorption of power and it wasn't something he consciously did.

When I refocused on the two of them, I had no more answers than they did.

"Maybe it's the angel's grace. Michael had said I had his and Naomi assumes I also have my father's, so it could be... disrupting the natural order," I said.

CJ burst out laughing. "Disrupting the natural order? Dude, your entire existence disrupts the natural order. We've dealt with a lot in our lifetimes, but the existence of vampires and demons and hellhounds and Lucifer isn't anything we're equipped to deal with."

"CJ," Steve said, his concentration focused on the backyard. "I've had to alter my beliefs more than once during my lifetime. This is just another window that's opened up. A god-awful one, but if we sit in denial and turn our backs on Damian, we're setting up the end of days." He turned from the glass.

CJ sent a glare in his direction.

"We've dealt with angels and ghosts, along with some of the most evil bastards on earth, so what's a few more?"

"All due respect, but after tonight, Naomi and I will find somewhere else to go."

"Why?" Steve asked.

"Look closely at my memories, the ones with Lucifer," I said, moving my gaze between the two of them, waiting as they did as I asked.

CJ blanched a little, but Steve just sighed and refocused on me.

"So?" he said.

"I was no match for him, even in shadow form, so how do you expect to beat him?"

CJ stood and put his hand out, his mind commanding me to fly into the wall. Nothing happened and his face turned red with effort. He dropped his arm to his side, his eyes going wide as he stared at me. *Jesus, you took it all.*

"I didn't. Try moving something else," I said.

He glanced at the coffee table, and it rose off the ground. The relief on his face made me smile. Then he turned his gaze to me.

"Are you consciously trying to stop me?" he asked, trying to dissect why his powers didn't work on me.

"No," I said and thought about it. "I mean, I heard the command and felt what I would categorize as a breeze, but nothing like what you envisioned in your head." I shifted my gaze to Steve. "When you demanded the gun, I felt compelled to give it to you, so that was a conscious choice to ignore your request."

"So you're immune," Steve ventured and traded a glance with CJ.

"If I'm immune, you can bet your ass Lucifer is too."

"I'm not so sure. I've pulled Ty back down to the earth," Steve said, triggering that memory.

"He's not an archangel, is he?"

"No," Ty's voice boomed in the quiet room.

"Then we can't assume your influence or powers or whatever you call it will affect him in any way. I'd rather err on the side of caution and assume that it can't. If I'm wrong, then it will be a pleasant surprise for all of us, but if I'm right, at least we'll be prepared with something else up our sleeves," I said.

"What about trying to trap him?" Steve asked, and even his guardian angel laughed.

"No. I don't want him within a hundred miles of Naomi."

The garage door swung open, and the chill pulled my attention away from the conversation. Tom and Raven stood just beyond the door and they were not alone. The terror in their eyes pulled the air from my lungs; and when two demons stepped through the door holding knives to their throats, the horror of coming here slammed home.

"Put the knife down," all three of us commanded, one voice, three wills, and the knives tumbled from the demon's hands.

The minute the immediate threat neutralized, Tom flipped the bastard holding him and Raven slammed her heel into the demon's foot, but he tightened his grip around her neck.

A white blur shot through the air, hitting the demon holding Raven, peeling him off her and leaving her shaking. Naomi's snarl drowned out the demon's dying screams. Tom grabbed Raven, pulling her to where we stood. I didn't wait for the second demon to react, instead, I tried to do exactly what CJ had willed to happen to me and I blinked in shock as the bastard flew into the wall, cracking the drywall and pulling Naomi's attention away from her dead catch.

"How did you find me?" I asked, and the bastard smiled, his gaze dropping to the cut on my leg. The cut made by a hellhound's teeth.

"You're marked," he said and laughed.

I roared with the anger filling my soul, willing the unthinkable.

Blood mist filled the room, and I blinked, staggering back a step before dropping to the couch. I didn't understand what just happened and Steve waved his hand in front of my gaze, pulling my attention away from the spot the demon had been. My ears buzzed and my gaze dropped to the massive tiger nuzzling my lap. Naomi's tongue ran a warm path across my cheek and she pushed into me again. I scanned her blood-soaked fur and looked up at Steve. He wore the same gory mess that the rest of us did.

"What happened?" I asked, looking from Steve to CJ and then beyond to Tom, holding Raven in his arms. My gaze transitioned from the people to the actual room and my mouth dropped open. Blood even dripped from the ceiling.

"You made him explode."

I turned toward CJ, meeting his horrified gaze, and then I looked beyond him at the pristine angel behind him.

"I did that to someone once," he said, glancing around the room and then back at me. "It's pretty fucking messy."

I let out a bark of a laugh.

"It happens when the juice gets away from you, and I'd say that's exactly what happened here."

Instead of dignifying his comment with an answer, I ran my fingers behind Naomi's ears, glancing up at Tom and Raven. "Where did they ambush you?"

"In the garage, after we got out of the car," Raven said.

"And you didn't warn us?" CJ glared at Tom.

"No time," he signed.

Naomi's ears flattened, and she hissed at the back door.

I turned and stared at the pack of hellhounds keeping watch.

"Fuck," I whispered and chanced a glance in Steve's direction.

He bolted for the training room, his fear hanging on the air and agitating the dogs outdoors. Jennifer argued with him until he pulled her into the family room and then she dropped silent, letting him move her beyond Naomi and me to where the rest of their family stood together.

It wasn't until the air outside shifted and the pack parted I felt the first threads of fear.

"Do you have salt?" I asked. A moment later, a container of Morton's salt appeared. I pulled my gaze away from the man standing amid the hellhounds and looked up at Steve. "Pour a line in front of the doors and on the windowsills. Now."

Steve crossed and laid a patch of salt across the floor in front of the sliders and then the garage door. He disappeared and did the same to the front door and the windowsills, coming back with a near empty container that he set on the counter.

I knew it wouldn't stop Lucifer, but it would stop demons.

The tap on the back window pulled all our gazes, and I stared into Lucifer's angry glare. He scanned the room and his expression turned to disgust, but it wasn't his face that had my attention. It was the wings. Lucifer came calling in his deadliest form.

Wings next to me fluttered into view and Ty Ryan appeared in full glory.

Lucifer bared his teeth at the angel next to me. "Uriel," he growled loud enough to hear through the glass.

Ty laughed, shaking his head. "Try again, asshole," he said.

Lucifer focused on Ty, his gaze narrowing

I met Steve's wide gaze. "Go," I whispered and nodded toward the stairs. "He can't get in and neither can anymore demons."

I wasn't so sure about the hellhounds, but they seemed to be held at bay for the time being. I grabbed the salt and lined the bottom stair, creating a buffer for the rest of the family.

Naomi hissed, pacing in the small space.

Lucifer snapped his fingers, and Ty's smile disappeared. Standing next to the devil was a bloodied and beaten man, his haunted eyes matching that of the angel standing next to me.

"Chris," he whispered, stepping forward.

I reached out and grabbed his arm, my fingers gripping solid flesh and not air like I expected. Ty looked down at my grip and then into my eyes. The window to his soul opened, and I saw even more than what I had gleaned from Steve.

The hellhounds surrounded Chris, toying with him. The first rip of flesh brought forth a soul-crushing scream and Ty struggled against my grip.

"That's my brother," he said.

"He's already dead," I said.

"So am I." He tried to yank from my grip.

"You can't save him." I met his irritated gaze, and I knew where his heart was, but he wasn't thinking straight, not with the brutal spectacle outside the glass. "You cannot open that door."

"I have to try," he said, tears filling his bright blue eyes.

"If he gets into this house, who do you think he'll kill first?"

Ty glared at me. "You."

I shook my head and suddenly the truth hit him and he dropped to his knees, remembering the dark period when he hung between life and death. He glanced up, pain filling his features as the hellhounds tore Chris apart in front of us.

"You can't kill a ghost," I whispered.

"No, but you can torture a soul for eternity," he replied, his voice filled with anguish.

I kept hold of his arm, watching the blood spill, the anger building, agitating Naomi and she charged at the glass, stopping short and putting her claws on the window.

It was a stupid move that exposed her belly, and I saw the hellhound lunge. It hit, cracking the glass into a spider-web fracture. Naomi leaped back, retreating to the spot in front of Ty and me.

"Naomi, go upstairs," I said, and she turned her head, baring her feral teeth. "Go," I whispered and pointed, ignoring her angry stare. I finally dropped my gaze. "I will be fine. I need you to protect our family." I didn't need to expand anymore, and she turned, heading upstairs like I requested.

The second dog hit the glass, sending shards our way. I still had a grip on Ty's arm and we traded a glance. "It's your house," I said, dropping my hand.

He looked around the room and then back at me.

"Vaporize the fuckers," he said, and the power surged in my chest.

His brother's screams bled through the glass and when another dog launched, I let loose.

Lucifer stepped back, shock filling his features and his gaze locked on the spot the hellhound had launched from. All that remained was a back paw; Lucifer was wearing the rest of the creature in a spray of blood and guts.

Lucifer wiped the blood off his face and looked at his hand before leveling a glare at Ty.

He wrongly assumed the angel had killed his hound. Neither of us corrected him, either.

Chris's screams had subsided, but the sound of flesh tearing still permeated the glass. Lucifer pointed to the decimated form. "This is now your brother's fate. He will suffer an eternity of being ripped to shreds by my dogs," he growled, and then his gaze turned to me.

"When I return, there will be nothing you can do to stop me and my army from getting to your precious wife."

In a blink, he was gone, and so were Chris and the dogs.

Ty hung his head. "That should have been me," he whispered.

I stood transfixed, my body trembling. The expenditure of energy didn't diminish the magic flowing in my bloodstream, instead, it magnified.

"Damian?" Naomi's voice cut through the waves of thought, and I glanced at my surroundings until my gaze landed on her at the base of the stairwell.

"He's coming back, and he's bringing... things with him." I didn't know if it would be demon or vampire or something else entirely, but no one in the house was safe. Not even the angel beside me kneeling in defeat.

Trinity Rising
Chapter Fifteen
Damian

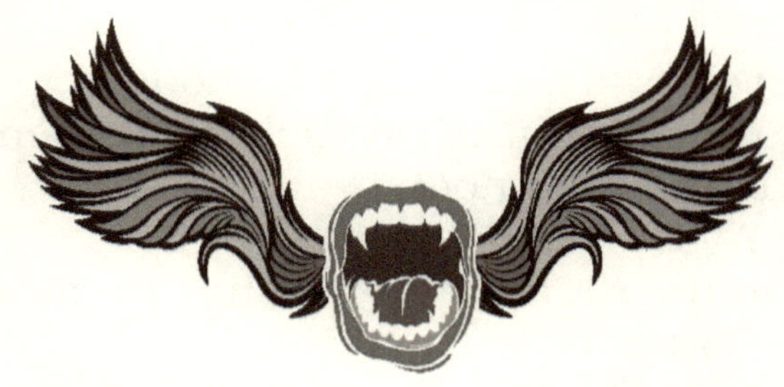

"HOW MUCH TIME DO we have?" Steve asked, swiping his clean face with a towel.

"I have no idea, but whatever he's bringing back..." I stopped and closed my eyes for a minute, thinking about some things I knew about Lucifer and the monsters he commanded. "If he brings vampires back, Naomi and I are safe, but you aren't." I met his gaze. "They can get through the symbols and salt and once even one symbol is compromised, Lucifer can get in."

"I thought you said there were no more vampires," he said.

I opened my mouth to speak and then just sighed. "I honestly don't know. I thought Eve was the last, but who the hell knows?"

"He said there were things far worse than vampires," Naomi said, meeting my gaze.

I bit my lip, thinking about what could be worse. "The only thing as deadly as a demon that can break through our defenses is a vampire." I stopped and spun, staring out the window at my car before digging into my pockets. I clasped the key, yanking it out.

"I trust you have a nine-millimeter?" I asked Steve.

His eyebrows arched and he nodded.

"Get the gun out of my jacket," I ordered and headed to the front door.

"Why?"

"Platinum rounds. Heart shot or head shot will kill a vampire."

I grabbed the salt as I passed and poured an arch wide enough for the door to swing open without compromising the integrity of the demon defense.

"What are you doing?" Naomi grabbed my arm as I reached for the door.

"Getting the ammunition from the trunk. Did you want me to grab my bag while I'm out there?" I hadn't brought anything in and we were all in need of changing out of the blood-soaked clothing.

She glanced down at her sodden outfit and nodded. Her stomach had grown enough to stretch the wet fabric. I wondered if my sweats would be enough and then swept the thought aside and swung the door open, stepping out into the quiet night.

I didn't mosey. In fact, I sprinted and popped the trunk when I was still a couple of paces away. Sweeping my hand through handles, I hauled the duffel bags over my shoulder and reached for the boxes of ammunition, sweeping them into one of the smaller environmental-friendly shopping bags. I reached for the top of the trunk and a low growl froze me in place. The feral sound rumbled from behind me and I held my breath, closing the trunk slowly before turning to face whatever was in the driveway.

"Fuck," I whispered as I stared at a beast that looked like a cross between a hellhound and a grizzly. I couldn't back up, so I took a step toward the house. The thing bared its teeth, snarling. A gunshot rang out, and the thing yelped. I didn't wait for it to react; I turned and sprinted toward the open door.

Steve stood on the front step, aiming at the thing behind me. I scanned the front of the house, making sure there wasn't another one of these creatures waiting to pounce. The ground shook, followed by another gunshot. My heart pounded in my chest and I wished for my vampire speed.

Inside. The thought ripped from my mind and Steve took another shot before retreating and holding the door wide. I dove the last few feet, flipping myself into a break-fall, and the door slammed closed before I rolled to my feet. I dropped everything and grabbed the salt as the beast hit the other side of the door. It held, and I drew a shaky line of salt across the entryway and took a step back before the tremors reduced me to a hyperventilating pile on the floor.

"What the hell was that?"

I glanced up at him, trying to catch my breath, and shook my head. Instead of trying to guess, I reached into the bag and tossed him a box of ammunition. "Nice shooting," I breathed.

Naomi stepped into view.

"I guess there are some things that are worse," I said and sat back on my ass, leaning my forearms on my knees, still huffing. I glanced at the gun in Steve's hand and then up at him. "That's not mine." I pointed my chin at the Sig Sauer in his hand.

"Tom has yours."

Steve put his hand out, and I took it, allowing him to help me to my feet. We stepped into the kitchen and I crossed to the refrigerator. I didn't ask like I should have, instead; I opened the door and pulled the first beer within reach. I could have used scotch, but something cold that would stop my hands from shaking without clouding my mind was more appropriate for the situation.

I guzzled half the beer before turning around. A layer of a shock bit at my skin. It looked like Mr. Clean had visited the family room, except for a two-foot diameter of blood on the floor and a few tendrils stretching across the room. CJ's head was bent in concentration as the last of the tendrils pooled together. He exhaled and opened his eyes.

"Now all we need are showers," he said.

I handed Naomi the duffel bags. "Women first," I said and got no argument from anyone. Naomi hesitated, her gaze bouncing between the window behind us and me.

"Go clean up." I didn't leave any leeway in my command and she nodded, following Jennifer and Raven up the stairs.

Tom still held the gun aimed at the sliders, even as I approached.

"Why don't you and CJ go cleanup, as well? I think Steve and I can handle it for a few minutes."

He turned, glancing at me, and then Steve, waiting for the okay. I glanced over my shoulder, but Steve wasn't looking at us. He was busy loading his gun with the new bullets, his gaze jumping from the front entry to the window.

Tom brought his gaze to me. "oo o," he said and his mind echoed the proper enunciation of "You go."

I glanced at CJ, and he gave me a nod. "We've got this."

"I'll only be a few minutes," I said and took the opportunity.

The guest room had a private bathroom, and I stepped into it, peeling off my clothing and dropping them on Naomi's pile. She spun when I opened the door and I paused.

"You got bigger," I said and slipped inside.

I didn't have time to study her swollen belly; instead, I moved her out of the warm spray with a mumbled apology and grabbed the soap, scrubbing as quickly as I could. I didn't even wait until the water ran clear before lathering up my hair and rinsing. She watched from just outside the spray, her arms crossed over her breasts in an effort to keep warm. When my hair squeaked beneath my fingers, I moved her back under the water and captured a kiss.

"Thank you," I whispered and then left her in the warm flow.

I toweled off and stalked into the bedroom, ripping open the darker duffel bag. A hodgepodge of clothing met my search, and I found underwear, an undershirt, and a pair of socks. After I pulled my undergarments on, I found a pair of jeans, sliding them on before grabbing a flannel shirt. I hesitated, glancing between the blood-ridden sneakers by the door and my stocking-clad feet. My work boots were still in the car and there was no way in hell I was going outside again. I jammed my feet into my sneakers and headed out of the bedroom, buttoning my shirt as I descended the stairs. It took me exactly five minutes from the time I entered the bedroom to the time I hit the landing and my heart hadn't stopped slamming the walls of my chest.

"Your turn," I said, hand combing my dripping locks away from my face before putting my hand out for the gun.

Tom nodded and handed over the weapon, slipping upstairs.

"Steve?" CJ asked, putting his hand out for Steve's gun.

"You go," he said.

"There isn't an open bathroom for me," CJ said, and Steve sighed, looking between his adopted son and me. "We can handle five minutes alone," CJ added.

"Fine." He handed over the gun and sprinted the same way I had.

CJ moved toward me, his gun trained on the front of the house, and I stood with mine on the back entry. He stopped at my shoulder and met my gaze. "You need to learn to control it," he said.

I started laughing and looked out at the darkness beyond the glass. The power he had transferred seemed to take on a life of its own inside me, snaking through my cells like a forest fire during a drought. My gaze dropped to my hands holding the gun, specifically the tremor in them. Fear didn't drive the shakes. The tornado inside me was responsible, and I glanced back at CJ.

"How?" I whispered.

He stared at me and then focused on the front again. "How did you control yourself when you were a vampire?"

"I didn't in the beginning," I admitted and shame painted my face with heat. "But I learned to feed when I had to and not just when the need struck. It was a delicate balance. And when they started storing blood, it made things much easier." I glanced at him and shrugged. "Scotch helped, too."

He grinned, his white teeth a stark contrast to the bloody streaks still present on his skin. The water went off overhead and he glanced at me. "Every time you use the destructive ability, it gets stronger and when you lose control, it blooms like a sun flare."

"You've never lost control," I said, thinking about his memories.

CJ shook his head. "No, I haven't. I came close a few times, but I was able to rein it in before I lost it. Let me leave you with something to consider. You took the equivalent of a raindrop compared to the ocean out there, and you're having a rough time controlling that small infusion. Can you imagine the damage that would result if I ever lost control?"

He met my gaze, and I shivered at the possibilities.

Naomi stepped into the room and glanced at the two of us before putting her hand out. "Our bathroom is free," she said and CJ glanced at her hand, raising his eyebrow in question.

"She's a better shot than I am," I said and he glanced at the ceiling, then at me before he relinquished the gun.

Naomi stepped next to me, adopting the same stance CJ had, her focus on the front window as he disappeared up the stairs. When her gaze met mine, she gave me a strained smile. I took the time to glance at her attire, sweats and an oversized t-shirt that stretched over her belly.

"I'm not going to have any clothes left, am I?" I said and refocused on the glass sliders, wondering if we'd get the chance to get maternity clothes. Her belly had grown disproportionately and at this rate, even my oversized bum-around sweats would be too small for her.

"They're the only thing that sort of fits at this point," she said and shifted. "Every time I change into the tiger, it's acting like an accelerant. The good news is I can feel the baby moving. A lot."

I dropped my left hand, placing it on her extended belly and a foot connected, pulling my attention from the glass back to her. The flurries within made me blink and stare at her stomach. I focused and let out a small laugh at the distinct, simplistic thoughts coming from inside.

"They're hungry," I said, raising my gaze to hers.

"They?"

"Yes, you are carrying more than one." I pulled my hand back to steady the gun, my heart feeling both lighter with the new knowledge and fiercer on my intent to defend my family.

"How do you know?" she whispered, her focus on me and not the window in front of her.

"Keep watch," I hissed, and her gaze went back to where it belonged.

"How many do you think?" she asked, even though her mind kept focusing on how I knew.

"Two," I said, analyzing the nuance of thoughts. "Maybe three," I added after a minute. I could identify two distinct voices, but there was an echo on one that made me think it might be three.

"Twins?"

I grinned and nodded. The stairs creaked, pulling my gaze for a moment. Tom and Raven descended into the room with a duffel bag and Naomi relinquished the gun to Tom when he extended his hand. A few minutes later, Steve and Jennifer came down.

"We need to leave," Steve said, and I raised an eyebrow.

"Yes," Jennifer said. "As soon as CJ is done, we need to go."

I nodded. I couldn't blame her. If I were in her shoes, I'd bail as soon as I could, too.

"We're not bailing on you. We're bringing you with us," Steve said, throwing a separate duffel bag on the floor.

"They can track me," I said. "At least that's what the demon said."

"Not where we're going."

The certainty in his voice made me sigh. "You've been wrong before," I pointed out.

"But I've never been wrong," Jennifer said. "Go get your bags. We only have a small window to get out of here."

"There's a demon bear outside. How do you suggest we get past it?" I stood my ground, dropping my gaze to Jennifer's.

She held up a controller. "Bears have sensitive hearing and we have a hell of a house alarm."

Her answer shocked me, and I handed Steve my gun, trotting upstairs and retrieving our bags. CJ met me in the hall with a backpack slung over his shoulder.

"I guess we're going on a road trip," he said.

As we filtered out, I glanced over my shoulder at the angel still standing in the house. With a swipe of my arm, I broke the symbol on the garage door and the angel popped out of sight.

A Tahoe occupied the third garage spot, and I smiled at the large vehicle. We each threw our bags in the back and then piled in. As soon as we had locked and closed all the doors, Jennifer and Steve exchanged a glance. A moment later, the garage door blew to pieces and the house alarm pierced the air.

I don't think I fully appreciated the power of a Chevy engine until this beast roared to life and we hit fifty before the gate blew off the hinges. When Steve's phone rang, he shook his head.

"Don't answer it. Let them send the cops," he said, and I couldn't help but laugh.

"Too bad you cleaned up the family room," I said over my shoulder. Meeting CJ's gaze. He smiled and closed his eyes for a second.

"That should keep the place crawling with people for quite a while."

I thought about my car and the electronics inside and bit my lip. As much as I loved the car, the cops couldn't start digging around in there, and I added to the melee. With controlled focus, I made my car explode, destroying all the electronics along with my prized car. A pang of sorrow hit and I pressed my lips together, watching the plume of smoke retreat into the distance.

"It's just a car," Naomi said, and I nodded, but it still felt like I had taken a gut shot.

"The mural..." I started, and she shook her head.

"I put it in my duffel bag," she whispered and squeezed my hand. "Maybe I'll be able to wear it like a poncho," she added and ran her hand over her stomach.

Jennifer turned in the front seat. "You look much bigger than you did earlier," she said.

Naomi just nodded. Neither of us understood the acceleration and as I gazed at her, I wondered what it was doing to her. I took a moment to study her and then I closed my eyes, listening to the hum of discontent coming from her abdomen. Soon, their demands would bloom into something Naomi would have to answer.

"I may have something you can wear at the cottage," Jennifer said, her gaze dropping to Naomi's belly, and a flash of sadness filled the car. She turned toward the front, staring out the windshield as Steve barreled down the road, his focus on getting us all to what he deemed a place of safety instead of his equally harsh pang of sorrow.

"The cottage?" Naomi asked.

"We own a cottage in New Hampshire. On Paradise Cove," Steve said and glanced in the mirror at me.

The name started a flow of memories. Paradise Cove seemed to be a mystical gateway, one where miracles happened, but I still didn't get why they were leading the devil to such a place. "Why there?"

"Because Paradise Cove will provide us with an army of our own," Jennifer said, turning and meeting my gaze. "An army equipped to bury your nemesis."

Trinity Rising
Chapter Sixteen
Naomi

A DEEP CHILL PENETRATED my body, and I shivered, glancing over at Damian. Ever since he shook CJ's hand, something in him had changed. I have no idea what happened with the demon, either. One minute, I was ripping the throat out of one of them and the next; the house was full of red mist. It was as if the bastards were wired with a ton of C-4, but the blast only affected the demons.

Damian leaned over. "I got a little of their magic," he whispered in my ear and kissed my cheek before pulling away.

"What does that mean?" I didn't intend to shout out the question, but he chuckled in response and Steve glanced back at me.

"It means your husband has been touched by more than just angel grace. He's the one who disintegrated those demons, and it was his display of power that made your car blow up like a fireworks disaster," Steve said. "And if I'm not mistaken, he can read your mind."

"But he doesn't have a good handle on controlling it yet," CJ said from the backseat.

I was getting more irritated by the second. It wasn't their words, but their tone, like they were handling me with kid gloves, like I wouldn't understand what they were saying, and I turned, meeting Raven's gaze.

"Do they always talk to women like they're feeble-minded?"

Raven pressed her lips together but didn't hide the snort of laughter. "Aye, especially when they talk about their gifts," she said, her Irish accent coming through with her full-bodied laugh. Tom rolled his eyes and shook his head, but he kept his mouth closed and his hands still. CJ glared at his sister-in-law and then at me.

"We don't think you're feeble-minded," he said. "It's just..."

"Dude, I was a vampire," I said, silencing everyone in the car. "When I get pissed, I turn into a fucking tiger. I've dealt with angels, killed demons and even danced with the fucking devil, so when you toss out lame descriptions for psychic occurrences, I get irritated." I glared at the three in the back and turned to the front, leveling the same disgust in the mirror at Steve. "I am a Mohegan warrior princess, and just because I'm a pregnant, hormonal wreck, doesn't mean you have to treat me like an unstable idiot."

"Mohegan warrior princess?" Damian chuckled, and my glare shot to him. He raised his hands, trying to show he meant no harm, but in his gaze, I saw the years of teasing I'd get for that statement.

I looked out the window, and a smile found my lips. Chuckles erupted from the front passenger seat along with the row behind me.

"My grandfather used to call me his warrior princess," I muttered and slid my gaze to Damian. I couldn't completely suppress my smile. He grinned at me and winked.

"Well, I'm glad you're my warrior princess," he teased in that endearing manner that made me alternate between wanting to slap him and kiss him.

"Damn, she's a pistol," Steve laughed, glancing at Damian.

He grinned and nodded. "Yes, she is," he said, oozing with pride.

Laughter filled the car, and in the midst of it, Steve's phone buzzed again. This time, he didn't ignore the call. He answered, and a panicked voice filled the car.

"Steve?"

"Hi, Sarah," he said and glanced at his wife.

"What the hell?" the woman said, and I smiled, picking up the distinct New York City accent.

"Where are you?" he asked, his laughter now fizzling out, replaced by worry lines.

"I'm on my way to your place. The police said it was a mess."

"Steer clear of there until I call you. It's not safe for anyone we give a damn about."

Silence came over the line and the sound of a car slowing to a stop replaced the hum in the background.

"Did you just admit to giving a shit about me?"

I watched the exchange between Jennifer and Steve before he sighed. There was a history there that piqued my curiosity.

"Yeah. I give a shit," he grumbled.

"Jen?"

"Hi, Sarah," Jennifer said.

"It's that fucking bad?"

Another exchange and then Jennifer glanced back at me as she answered. "Worse than you can imagine, but we're all alive and breathing, so..."

"You know I can't just make excuses and not show up."

"If she has to go, tell her to steer clear of anyone she doesn't know. And don't say anything about talking to us," I said, staring at Jennifer. "Otherwise, you'll never see her again."

"Who the hell is that?" Sarah barked and after that, she said, "Is that the girl from the hospital? Did you find those two psychos?"

"I found them," Steve said, giving me the keep-your-mouth-shut glare. "Trust me on this one," he added.

"And who the hell did they kill? There's blood all over your family room and on the lawn in the backyard, according to the call we got."

"They didn't kill anyone."

I met his gaze in the mirror. He lied better than I expected from a federal agent.

Damian leaned close. "He worked undercover for years," he whispered, his voice tickling my ear. I glanced at him and then my gaze drifted beyond.

Headlights were too close.

"Watch out!" I screamed just as the Ford truck slammed into the side of the Tahoe and we swerved. The back wheel caught dirt and slid, swinging around and then nothing. No sound at all as the vehicle started the beginning of a death roll.

Trinity Rising
Chapter Seventeen
Naomi

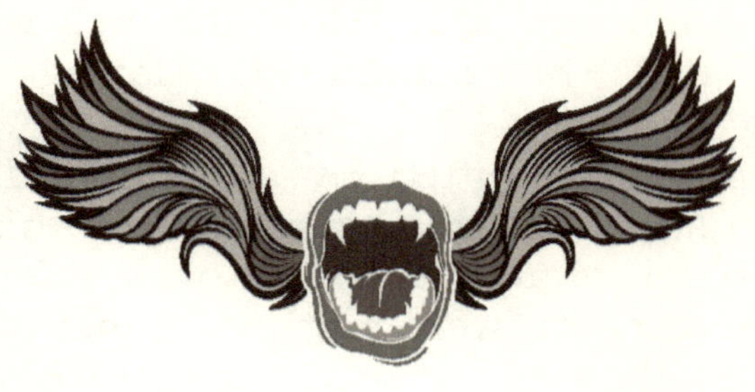

IMAGES REGISTERED BETWEEN BLINKS, and my entire body tensed, waiting for the impact.

The crazed smile of the demon driver who ran us off the road.

The Ford flashing over in a ball of flame and then turning to dust.

Cars swerving to avoid hitting us.

We spun in the air and I could no longer see the traffic behind us. I expected shattered glass and crumpling metal. I expected the jar of the seatbelt and the following whiplash. I didn't expect what happened.

The vehicle completed the revolution, and the tires bounced on the asphalt, finding purchase and propelling us forward.

Cars braking around us were louder than our impact. The only sound was our collective breathing, hard and laborious, like we all had just run the hundred-yard dash.

"What the hell was that?" Sarah roared on the speakerphone.

"I hit a guardrail," Steve answered. "I'm going to have to call you back," he added and disconnected the call. "How the hell are they finding us?" he demanded, glaring in the rearview mirror.

"Damian was bitten by a hellhound earlier today," I said and dropped my gaze to his leg. "I think that's what the demon was referring to when he said you were marked." I met his stark stare and then his gaze dropped to his leg as well. His expression altered, and he closed his eyes.

"Did anyone think to grab the salt?" he asked and silence met his question.

"What were you going to do, pour salt in your cut?"

"Yes. I figure if salt keeps demons out, it might mask my whereabouts."

"Do we need to stop?" Steve asked.

"There isn't time," Jennifer said.

The bouncing conversation along with the erratic lane changes were making me sick, and I swallowed the acidic taste in my mouth.

"We might need to stop anyway," Damian said and brushed a stray hair behind my ear. "Naomi needs to eat."

"I'll be fine," I muttered, but if I didn't eat soon, I was going to pass out or vomit. The pizza I had before the demons attacked had long been digested and absorbed and the babies were starting to kick.

"You need food," Damian said, and his gaze fell on my stomach. "The dinner you ate wasn't enough to fuel your transformation, never mind the accelerated growth of the babies."

Jennifer glanced over her shoulder. "How far along are you, anyway?"

I laughed and met her gaze. "I'm supposed to be due in October."

Her eyebrows arched and she dropped her gaze to my stomach. Her lips moving silently, forming partial words before she looked back at me. "That means you're a little less than two months?"

I nodded. "I was less than two months before I transformed, but I have no clue how far along I am now. And Damian thinks we're having twins."

"Triplets," CJ and Jennifer said at the same time, and I met her gaze while Damian looked back at CJ.

"How do you know?" I asked Jennifer.

She offered me a strained smile and traded a glance with Steve. "I had a vision."

Even Damian looked surprised with the answer, but he quickly recovered, and his hand found my belly. He caressed my abdomen and smiled. "You need to eat, because they are still hungry."

"I need to get gas anyway," Steve mumbled and veered off toward the next exit. When we stopped, Damian helped me out of the car and I wobbled into the convenience store, heading directly into the bathroom.

"You guys have to calm down. I'm going to get something to eat just as soon as I can," I said, rubbing the swollen skin. Once I had relieved the pressure on my bladder, the babies calmed, almost as if they shared in my relief. I shimmied the sweats back up and stepped to the sink.

My reflection took me by surprise and I stared at my gaunt face and ringed eyes. I hadn't had the time to inspect what I looked like at the house, but I never imagined I looked this bad. No wonder I felt like death.

"Damian?" I said, and the door opened.

"Are you okay?" he asked.

"Look at me." I pointed to the mirror. "I look like a walking skeleton."

He sighed and nodded. "I know. You need to eat."

"No shit," I responded and grabbed a paper towel, wiping my hands before tossing the crumpled paper into the garbage. "No wonder the guy at the counter looked at me like I was a fucking ghost," I muttered and stepped out into the heart of the store.

As I walked by the candy shelf, a hunger pain hit and I doubled over, holding my stomach. My insides felt like a hand was squeezing, trying to make my stomach pop like a balloon, and my knees gave out, hitting the hard floor. I couldn't draw a breath.

I didn't understand what was happening and I couldn't call out.

"Is she okay?" the kid at the counter called.

"She will be," Damian said and swept me up into his arms, carrying me toward the door while I forced small breaths. His gaze bounced, like he was looking for the cause, and then he stopped, pulling me closer. The car wasn't at the pump and the man standing in the darkness beyond the station lights made my stomach clutch tighter.

Lucifer.

Pain seared through me, and I screamed, fighting the darkness threatening to pull me into oblivion.

Trinity Rising
Chapter Eighteen
Naomi

TIRES SQUEALED AND THE Tahoe slammed to a stop in front of us, blocking my view of the bastard pulverizing my insides. The back door swung open and Damian climbed in with me in his arms. Before we even settled in the seat, the door closed, pulled by whatever psychic magic the men in the car possessed. Steve gunned the engine, and I had a moment to capture Lucifer's angry glare as we sped off. The farther away we got, the looser the tightness in my abdomen became.

I hyperventilated, leaning over as far as my oversized stomach would allow, and slowly, my seized lungs released, allowing oxygen to flow until the pain finally abated.

"Why isn't he following?" I asked when I had my voice back.

"I painted the symbols on the ceiling." Steve pointed to the roof of the car and I looked up.

The deep red etched in the gray fabric pulled a gasp from my throat. "Is that blood?"

"Yes," he answered and raised his left hand. I caught the make-shift bandage wrapped around his palm. "It's all we had." He glanced in the mirror, meeting my gaze for a moment. "I'll swing into the drive through somewhere in Brooksfield for you. It won't be much longer. Okay?"

I nodded, despite the incessant rumbling in my stomach.

"Maybe you should drop me off on the side of the highway and take her somewhere safe," Damian said.

I shot an open-mouthed gape in his direction and shook my head. "No! You're not going to be a martyr this time. You've done that too many times before, and every time you decide to make the sacrifice, you come within a hair's breadth of death. It's not happening again."

"But..." he started.

"No," I growled through clenched teeth. The prickling of the transition started, and I pushed it back. I didn't have room to transition in the car and I certainly didn't want to find out how far along I'd be when I snapped back to human form.

"Naomi, it's dangerous for me to be here. I'm the damned magnet that leads them right to us every time."

"You need to be with us, Damian," Steve said. "You're the only one who can stop that maniac."

"CJ could stop him," Damian argued, and I gave him a sideways glance, trying to understand what made CJ Ryan so special, beyond his uncanny similarity to my husband.

"He can't," Ty's detached voice said. "Even on hallowed ground, he's still doesn't have the power to kill the devil."

Fear flashed over Damian's features and he swallowed, dropping his gaze. I didn't have to be a mind reader to know he was replaying every brutal encounter with Lucifer. When he looked out the window, his jaw tightened, followed by his grip on my hand.

The minute his gaze came back to mine, I shivered at the raw fury filling his bright-blue eyes.

Damian's anger filled the car and instead of hitting it head on like I normally would, I curled up on the seat, putting my head in his lap. My stomach had turned to a roiling mess, and I needed a little tender loving care.

He sighed and started slowly hand combing my hair. The triplets had started doing acrobatics in the small space and my back ached from the strain. I just wanted a normal pregnancy and a quiet life raising my children with Damian.

I wanted peace.

My eyelids closed under his continued pampering, and he started singing for my benefit. Soft and sweet, pulling me under the blanket of sleep.

Trinity Rising
Chapter Nineteen
Naomi

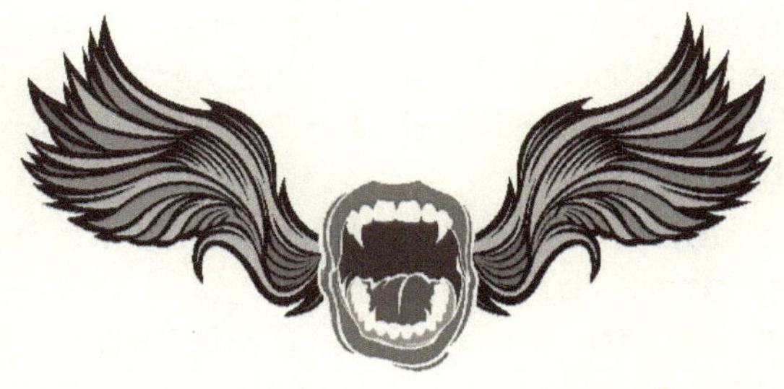

FRENCH FRIES.

The identification of the scent immediately popped me into a sitting position. I have no idea how long I was out, but now I was fully awake and ravenous. A quick glance at my surroundings told me we were in the drive through line of a Wendy's and my mouth salivated.

"What would you like?" Steve asked, meeting my gaze.

"Everything," I said in all seriousness, and he arched a brow. "Fine," I sighed and looked at the approaching board. "Two double bacon cheeseburgers, no, make that three, two large fries, a large chocolate frosty." I scanned the menu. "And maybe spicy chicken sandwich," I added. "Wait, make that three portabella bacon cheeseburgers instead of the double cheeseburgers," I said and smiled. "And a large frosty shake along with the chocolate frosty."

Steve stared at me in the mirror.

"That should do for me," I said and glanced at Damian. "Do you want anything?"

Damian snorted laughter and Steve looked down so I wouldn't see him grin. After the chortle of laughter filled the car, everyone yelled out their orders.

"Just hold on a second," he said as he rolled up to the drive through kiosk.

"Welcome to Wendy's. What can I get you today?" the chipper voice asked.

Steve accurately recounted my order, which impressed the hell out of me, and he continued ticking off what everyone had called out down to the last frosty. It was an impressive list for seven people, but no one had near the volume of food I ordered.

"I got this," Damian said, reaching for his wallet, but his expression fell when his hand came up empty. "Fuck," he muttered, and Steve glanced back at him. "My wallet was in the jeans I had on earlier," he said. "Which are on the floor in the bathroom upstairs."

"That means they're going to assume you had something to do with the disappearance of my family," Steve mumbled, pulling his wallet out and peeling off enough cash to cover the bill at the window.

We didn't linger. The minute the food was in the car and accounted for, Steve pulled out of the parking lot, heading down one of the main thoroughfares right through the middle of a college campus. He pushed the redial button on his phone as soon as he was sure no one was following us.

"Steve?"

"You went to the house, didn't you?" he asked, his voice filled with instant irritation.

"It's my job. There's blood everywhere. What the hell happened?" Sarah snapped back.

"We are all okay."

"You said that earlier. But after seeing this, clearly, someone isn't."

"Something. Not someone."

"What the fuck am I supposed to do with that?"

"Let it go. This is one of those situations where you don't want to know. Just like you don't want to know what the hell happened at the hospital in Torrington. It's way too out there for you to come to terms with."

Silence cascaded on the line.

"More fucked up than your guardian angel?"

"Far more," he said, his voice softening. "It's even more fucked up than what happened at Black Cove."

Jennifer shivered at the mention of Black Cove, encircling herself with her arms as if that could ward off whatever chill accosted her. I traded a glance with Damian and focused on my food, carefully unwrapping the first burger.

"Fine. Can I at least tell Ron that you're okay?"

"Go ahead," Steve answered. "And let him know that video didn't carry the full story. The man in the video was there, but he isn't responsible for those deaths. It's a setup. And I know who is responsible."

"Fine, I'll tell him," Sarah said, and the line went dead.

I tore into my second burger and glanced at Damian. I had a few questions, but my mind focused back on the food and I devoured it with zest, like this was my last meal.

Silence blanketed the car, and I looked up at Damian. His lips pressed together in derision and his gaze jumped between the food in my hands and my face and then he shook his head, taking a spoonful of my chocolate frosty that he held for me.

I glanced in the back and all three of them were staring at me in the same manner as Damian.

"I'm hungry," I said around a mouthful of French fries.

That seemed to break their morbid curiosity, and they all looked down at their own food. I glanced back at Damian. "What?"

"Wild dogs," he whispered and grinned, shaking his head like I was a hopeless case. He handed me my frosty and broke into his meal.

I finished mine before he had the chance to drink half his soda.

We pulled off the main road onto an overgrown dirt path between drifts of snow. I hadn't noticed the shift in the scenery from the snow dusted seacoast to the mountains of New Hampshire until now.

"Where are you taking us?" I asked and covered a burp. The triplets seemed to be falling into the same food coma I was entering, and I yawned.

"Paradise Cove," Steve said just as the woods opened to a clearing with a charming oversized cottage like the ones you'd see the rich and famous slumming in.

The moonlight reflected on the snow and Steve slowed as the garage opened and he pulled inside, throwing the car into park and cutting the engine. He waited until the door closed behind us before he reached up and scratched a line through the symbol, rendering it useless. Steve stepped out of the car and opened the door for me.

"You've got just enough time to hit the bathroom and then we have to move," he said, unlocking the house and waving me inside. The crew unloaded, but no one else came inside with Steve and me.

I did my business and stepped back into the dark room.

"You and Damian will need these," Steve said, handing me a down coat and once I pulled it on, he handed me the one for Damian and I stepped back into the garage.

Damian stepped close, and I offered him the coat. He slipped it on and we waited for Steve. A couple of minutes later, he came out with a metal box along with four coats draped across the top. After handing the coats to Jennifer, Raven, Tom and CJ, Steve set the box down and pulled out his keys.

"Get the ammunition," he said, nodding toward the back of the truck where Damian had stashed the grocery bag of bullets. Damian stepped to the trunk while Steve unlocked the box and handed CJ and Tom two of the revolvers from within the case. When Damian returned, he handed each one of them a box of ammunition.

"Load up, boys," Steve said and took a box himself, making sure his clip was full.

Damian did the same, and I watched each of the platinum bullets fit neatly in the clip and then he pushed it in place, meeting my gaze.

"You ready for this?" he asked me and I nodded, running my hands over my belly.

He offered me a strained smile and leaned down, meeting my lips with his cool ones.

"If something happens to me, make sure they know I loved them as much as their mamma," he whispered and pulled away.

"I hate it when you do that," I snapped. "Nothing's going to happen to you." I straightened, sending a glare in his direction before turning to Steve. "You got another gun?"

"I'm sorry, I don't," Steve answered, showing me the empty case. "Besides, you've got an advantage the rest of us don't."

"The tiger?"

He nodded.

"I'm not so sure that's a good idea," I said, running my hand over my belly.

"It's your best option if the shit hits the fan," he said.

As much as I didn't like that answer, I had to agree. I was a force in tiger form, especially after what I did to the hellhounds in the garage. I gave him a nod and moved next to Damian.

Steve checked the safety on the gun before stepping toward the door. He waited until everyone finished loading their clips, his gaze settling on each one of us as we lined up behind him.

"Game on," Steve said.

All the hairs on the back of my neck stood up. He opened the door, and I clamped my teeth together, steeling myself for battle.

Trinity Rising
Chapter Twenty
Damian

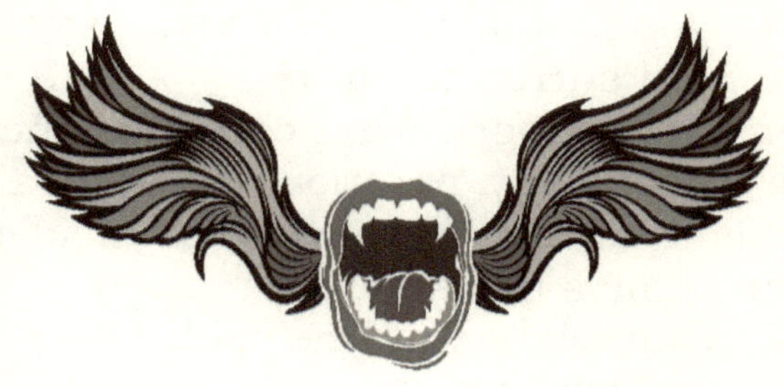

STEVE TOOK THE FRONT with the three women between us and Tom and CJ were at my back. The formation moved as one toward the woods. Each step left a crunching sound as we padded across the snow. Darkness surrounded us, but the moon shone brightly enough to make out shadows on the white landscape. Steve led us quickly onto a narrow path in the woods. The proximity of the trees made my imagination flare. This was the type of pathway I used to like to trap my victims on. With such little room for maneuvering, the victim wouldn't be able to put up much of a fight.

"Give me some credit," Steve said and glanced over his shoulder.

"It's the perfect place for an ambush," I replied, glancing around at the deep wooded boundaries. Muscles in my back tightened in response to the warning bells in my stomach.

Steve picked up the pace, and I glanced behind me, making sure Tom and CJ were still with us.

"We're good," CJ said, his voice soft, falling with the wind surrounding us.

When I turned forward, I could see the woods opening up and my paranoia dropped a notch. We made it to the glen without incident and Steve threw me a canister.

"Make yourself useful," he said.

I raised an eyebrow. "Salt?"

"Yes, make a barrier at the wood line."

"I'm not sure this is going to work," I said, but stepped to the path we just crossed over and poured a thick line across the snow-covered ground, continuing to the frozen water line of the small inlet. I crossed and did the same around the remainder of the perimeter until I shook the last grains of salt out of the container at the opposite shoreline and turned to the group.

"Now what?" I asked.

Steve traded a glance with Jennifer and then started clearing a space with his feet. "Now we make a fire and wait," Steve said. CJ and Tom helped clear the snow off with their feet, revealing a deep green moss that seemed to cover the entire opening.

"You know, for such a brilliant investigator, you can be a complete idiot," I said, and Steve looked up at me. "Step aside." I crossed to a spot just inside the salt line and pushed with my mind, clearing all the snow from the ground and the water, leaving a pile at the far edge of the icy cove.

Steve crossed his arms, glaring at me like I just did a major faux pas.

"What? You've got the power to do this. Why the hell would you do it manually?" I said and moved my gaze to Naomi. Her eyes were wide with awe. I guess she really didn't understand the powers this family harbored. I offered her a smile and a shrug.

"Because it reminds me I'm human, and not some all powerful god," Steve answered, his tone as sharp as his gaze.

I huffed and took a step forward, but something gripped the collar of my jacket, pulling my legs out from under me, and I was yanked backwards into the woods. Naomi's warning followed me into the darkness and I had a moment to flash to a bad horror movie I once saw. It snapped out of my head the moment I hit a tree, knocking the wind out of my chest. Dazed, I stared at a set of fangs dipping toward my neck.

I blocked the bite with my arm, but the beast's teeth sank into my flesh. I roared at the sting, but it was nothing compared to the vampire's scream. I hadn't had the pleasure of seeing what the cure did to a vampire before, like Naomi had, and the frothing blood bubbling from his throat was enough of a view. She hadn't been kidding when she said the cure ate vampires from the inside out. Horrified, I backed away a few steps, then turned and bolted toward the clearing, silently announcing to CJ and Steve that I was okay before breaking through the wood barrier. The burn of the bite faded as my blood flowed, cleaning the puncture wounds, but I was left with a dull throbbing ache.

Naomi stood on all fours, blocking the rest of the group, her growl sending a warning through the woods. I stopped a few steps inside the line and looked down at my arm. Blood dripped from my hand and Naomi's expression changed. Even on a tiger, I saw the concern.

"I'm fine," I said to her, although my heart still hammered from the adrenaline rush that fear afforded me. "I can't say the same for the vampire."

I looked up at the huddled group, Naomi in front and then the three men, guns drawn and pointing in three different directions. Jennifer and Raven stood behind them with the lake at their heels. Even Ty made an appearance, standing in the center of the ice, raining light on the dark alcove.

I crossed to Naomi, and she licked my hand, cleaning off the dark drips before nuzzling her head against my leg.

"It's probably a good idea that you stay in tiger form," I said and crouched down. "I think you can protect yourself better like this." Her tongue swathed my face, and I gave her a hug before pulling back. I stripped the coat and inspected my punctured arm. The bastard's teeth had gone into the meaty flesh of my forearm, but at least he hadn't torn a chunk out.

"Jesus," Steve muttered, and I looked up.

His gaze scanned the woods behind me and I turned, pulling the jacket back on and digging the revolver out of the pocket. At least a dozen vampires stepped into view, brought forward by the smell of my blood. While Naomi and I were immune to the virus, the others weren't, and a bite meant a highly unpleasant death.

They stopped, collectively smiling.

"The great Damian Andreas," one of them growled, and I focused on him. The face looked familiar, like someone I'd met in passing, but it didn't matter when or where. I had to rid the earth of these monsters, otherwise they'd keep multiplying.

"I'll give you to the count of three to leave. Otherwise, you'll be burning in hell before you can blink." I raised the gun, pointing it at a spot on the bastard's forehead. Naomi growled at my side and I heard the click of the safety on all the guns behind me.

Burn them. Torch their asses when I get to three, understand? I sent the thought out to Steve and CJ and got a resounding *Got it* from both of them.

"One," I said and paused when the vampires laughed.

"You're going to shoot us?" the lead asshole said and chuckled. "You should know better."

I smiled, looking over the gun. "Two, and yes, I know better," I said, and his cocky stance waned.

"Platinum?" he gasped and took a step back, fear transitioning his features from shadow back to the pale white of Lilith's brood.

"And we're all expert shots," I said and didn't wait for them to attack or retreat. Instead, I yelled, "Three!"

A wave of heat passed by me, joining with the power that leaped from my core, fanning out to encompass the mass of vampires. The stench of burned flesh filled the air, along with the dust of the decimated vampires.

Trinity Rising
Chapter Twenty-one
Damian

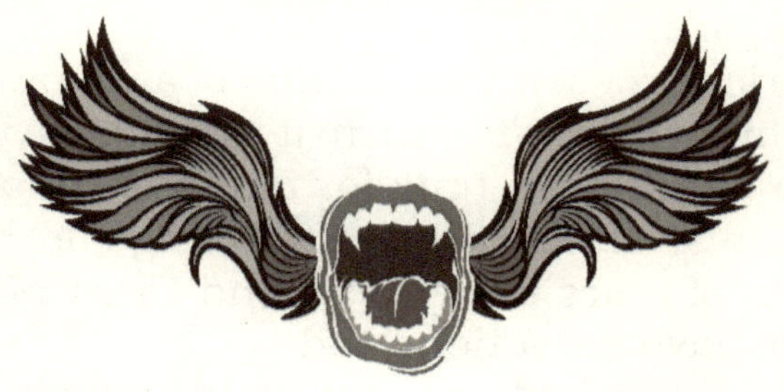

ASHIFT IN THE wind blew the dust into the woods and I turned, my heart lurching at the sight before me. Ty stood on the ice, surrounded by a host of angels. I stared at the assembly and my gaze locked on one pair in particular.

Michael stood revived in his youthful form but without wings. Beside him stood a similar wingless angel with a face I barely remembered, but one that made my arms drop to my side.

"μπαμπάς?" I asked in my native tongue. "Papa, is that really you?" My throat closed around a lump that formed. I hadn't seen my father since I was little and the fact he stood ready to do battle at my side pulled at my heartstrings.

The emotions that flew through my body left me numb. All the wrongs I had done flushed me with shame, and all the heroic actions counteracted, and I dropped my gaze to the ground, not knowing how to react.

"Damian," he whispered, and just his voice triggered fond memories of fishing on the banks of the Mediterranean. "My son," he added, and I met his gaze.

Gabriel crossed the distance and pulled me into a hug. I didn't return it right away, aware that we didn't have time for family reunions, but the warmth of the arms encircling me brought the burn of tears to my eyes and I met Michael's gaze. He gave me a tight nod.

"How?" I asked, scanning the white-winged beings in our midst, two of which were supposed to be trapped behind the gates of heaven.

Two who had sacrificed their grace for me.

Steve cleared his throat, and I pulled away from my father.

"I promised you an army," Steve said and waved his hand at the heavenly host, grinning like he knew a particularly intriguing secret.

Trinity Rising
Chapter Twenty-two
Damian

MOVEMENT PULLED MY ATTENTION back to the woods and a chill lit up the area, pressing down on me. I moved away from my father, closer to Naomi. A solid line of demons stepped into view, stopping at the salt line I poured.

The next wave of assailants took up their posts, side by side with a legion of hellhounds. Naomi actually stepped back at the numbers and I felt her fear. It blended with my own and one look at Steve and his family revealed they were in the same place we were.

Terror gripped every one of us and we spread out on the shoreline far enough away from the woods to be safe for the moment. Steve took the left side, and I took the right. CJ stood dead center. Jennifer, Tom and Raven stood a step behind, relying on us to provide a solid wall of defense. I glanced down at Naomi and pointed for her to join them. She hissed at me, but obeyed my silent command to move back.

Angels flanked us, providing a solid line between the innocents behind us and the demon horde. My heart scrambled in my chest, pumping a beat that nearly seized my lungs and I traded a glance with CJ. He swallowed and curled his hands around his revolver, aiming it at the closest demon.

The air sparked with tension and when the demons blocking the path parted; I knew we were in for a nasty battle. Lucifer stepped inside the ring, swiping a clean path through the salt I had laid down, and he wasn't alone.

He dragged a beautiful blonde woman forward, tossing her at his feet in front of him. When she raised her bruised face, Steve cursed under his breath and the gun moved from the line of demons to Lucifer.

Lucifer just grinned at the assembly and his black wings fluttered as he cracked his fingers. His gazed moved over the crowd of angels. "What have we here?" he said, scanning the line until his gaze landed on Gabriel and Michael. He tilted his head in contemplation, and then his gaze moved back to Steve.

"This lovely police officer was particularly useful," he said, meeting Steve's glare and waving his hand in the woman's direction.

Her gaze bounced from the demons surrounding us to the angels in line, landing on the tiger behind me. Then they jumped to Steve.

"What the fuck?" she whispered and Steve offered her a half laugh.

"I told you not to go to the house," he said, and I knew exactly who this was. The abrasive FBI agent Steve had spoken to on the phone. Sarah. Lucifer reached for the woman, grabbing a handful of her hair.

"Let go of me, asshole," Sarah snapped, swatting at his hand. While her voice was defiant and full of moxie, her eyes held a soul-crushing fear that I knew all too well.

He pulled her to her feet, bringing her close to him. Her elbow connected with his stomach, and he chuckled in her ear.

"I like my women feisty," he purred in her ear, keeping his gaze locked on Steve's. This primer was just the beginning of his dance, and I knew the woman was doomed.

We were all doomed.

"I'll tell you what," he said, running a sharp nail lightly down her arm. "I'll let you and your family go, along with this lovely officer, if you leave us to settle our differences," he said, nodding toward Naomi and me, negotiating a deal that would seal me in my grave.

I didn't move, but I made a point of recounting this beast's broken promises. The moment they stepped outside this cove, the hellhounds would tear them to bits.

"That includes leaving the angel and his son," Lucifer clarified, his gaze landing on Ty, narrowing into a hateful expression that I was used to receiving.

Steve's jaw clenched and his gaze dropped to Sarah.

"Do your magic and get me out of this," Sarah said, the panic reaching her voice as Steve's head shook back and forth.

His entire being shook and the frustration and anger pulsing in his veins drifted over me.

"You bastard," I whispered, and Lucifer sent a chilling smile in my direction.

"I can't do that," Steve said, and I glanced at him. Jennifer's hand rested on his shoulder and her forehead rested between his shoulder blades, her form shaking with silent sobs; and pain flashed in my chest.

I should have never let Naomi talk me into coming to Maine. We should have run across the globe, and then these pure souls wouldn't have to sacrifice those they loved for me.

CJ slid a glare in my direction and the mental reprimand resounded in my head like one of those obnoxious air horns. *Stop the fucking pity party.*

I winced at the volume and my gaze dropped to the ground, returning to the woman struggling in Lucifer's grasp.

Lucifer's hand ripped the shirt open, revealing a modest sports bra, and he tilted his head, smiling as his fingernails dimpled the skin over her heart. "Last chance," he said.

"I'm sorry, Sarah," Steve said, his eyes filled with tears and his lips pressed together.

Sarah's scream shattered the night, followed by the report of a gun. Smoke drifted from the end of Steve's revolver and I stared at it before turning toward the deafening silence.

Lucifer's fingers were buried knuckle deep in Sarah's chest, but that's not what silenced her scream. The neat bullet hole between her eyes had sent her to heaven before Lucifer could rip her heart out.

I turned back toward Steve, and his arms lowered. His chin dropped to his chest, and his breath hitched once. With a violent shake of his head, his tear-stained glare landed on Lucifer and the gun rose back in place.

"Get the fuck off my property," he said with a growl.

"As soon as I have my whore," he said.

Steve pulled the trigger again, but this time nothing happened until he moved the aim to the demon closest to Lucifer and then the gun jumped to life, expelling another round. The shot was as true as the one that took Sarah's life, and the first demon fell.

Lucifer yanked his hand from Sarah's flesh and tossed her next to the dead demon. He licked his fingers and scowled, glaring at Steve. The minute he stepped forward, Ty interceded, blocking the devil's path.

That hateful glare reappeared and Lucifer snapped his fingers, Christopher Ryan appeared in the center of the clearing, bleeding and on his knees, his screams filling the silent woods, echoing on the dark lake and the hellhounds tasked with ripping him to shreds continued their attack.

This time, Ty moved; his face filled with a wrath I had only seen once before and my gaze drifted to Michal. CJ took a step toward his father, pulling my attention back to the spectacle before us. Both Steve and I grabbed an arm, keeping him from entering the violent scene in front of us. This was the primer to the war, and I knew it was just an appetizer meant to drive the hounds in line into a frenzy, preparing them for attack.

"You can't stop it," I said when CJ tried to rip out of my grasp.

He turned a pleading gaze in my direction when the first hellhound turned on Ty.

I knew the pain in his gaze. I knew the need to stop the inevitable, and I also knew the futility of any action against what had already been set into motion.

What I didn't expect was for Ty to rip a hellhound in two with his bare hands and from the expression on Lucifer's face, neither did he.

Ty grabbed Chris around the waist and launched toward the heavens, pulling his brother out of range of the hellhounds into the single beacon of light, disappearing from view before Lucifer could yank him back to the earth.

Lucifer's furious gaze dropped from the sky to me, then moved to CJ. His face crinkled and he roared his aggravation, squeezing a fist in front of him, sending out the command to burst the boy's heart. I stepped into the flow of power aimed at Ty's son, deflecting it with a mental wall. Three of the demons next to Lucifer burst, exploding into balls of flame.

The surprise of the back-to-back events stunned everyone, and nothing moved until a streak of lightning flared and Ty landed on one knee in the center of the clearing like Thor arriving for battle. His wings smoldered, sending tendrils of smoke into the air, but when he lifted his head, his fury filled the space and he stood, shifting into a battle stance.

"You've cheated me for the last time," Lucifer growled and pointed at Ty.

"Game on, you bastard," Ty said and leveled the glare I had seen in Steve's mind. The one that dubbed the man as the Angel of Death while he was alive, and it evoked a tremor, a chill that bit at my heels and spread like a four-alarm fire.

Naomi hissed behind me, and the spell that held me in place broke. I remembered the gun in my hand and raised it, aiming at the closest hellhound. I squeezed the trigger and the report of gunfire shattered the stillness, breaking the stalemate between good and evil.

Trinity Rising
Chapter Twenty-three
Damian

THIRTY DEMONS WENT DOWN in the span of the ten seconds it took the four of us to empty our guns and the only one that took the time to re-load was Tom. The angels charged forward meeting the advancing demons in the center, but Steve, CJ and I stayed put, protecting our families behind us.

When Tom stepped between CJ and me, leveling the gun at the melee, I pushed his hand down and shook my head.

"Hold on to those. We might need them," I said, meeting his gaze and pushing him back into the safety of the cocoon we created.

A hellhound launched at us, and I let a targeted power bolt loose. The beast exploded, like the one at the house, and CJ and I traded a glance. I wasn't sure I could target only demons in the battle, but both Steve and CJ nodded.

"We have to try it," Steve said.

"On three," CJ said, and I closed my eyes, concentrating. "One," CJ breathed low over the bellows of fighting angels and demons.

"Two," I said and felt the tight coil in my chest.

"Three!" Steve said.

My eyes snapped open, and the wave rolled across the field, leaving only a bloody mist in its wake, along with four stunned angels.

Ty glanced at the three of us with a maniacal grin.

Lucifer stood at the edge of the field, scanning the gory remains of his army.

Michael and Gabriel stared at the mess with open mouths.

Only the sound of blood rain filled the space and I realize we'd annihilated demons and angels alike. Only archangels remained and my gaze landed on Ty. A shiver caught my soul, turning my blood as cold as the frigid water behind me.

We moved closer to Ty, Michael and Gabriel, squaring up to Lucifer, but he wasn't done with his arsenal of tricks. Naomi howled, and I blinked down at the writhing cat before my gaze jumped to Lucifer.

I charged without thought and got one hit in before his backhand hit me, spinning me onto the ground. The howl turned into an ear-piercing scream, snapping my gaze to my wife. Naomi lay in a ball, in human form, holding her stomach, screaming in pain.

The black power moved from Naomi to CJ, dropping him to his knees as he held his chest. His head dipped and his hands balled into fists.

When he snapped his gaze from the ground back at Lucifer, the devil stumbled back, nearly falling on his ass.

CJ stood, his breath coming in shallow bursts, and I scrambled to my feet, retreating to Naomi and falling on my knees next to her. She turned her head and shock filtered through me at the gaunt face that peered at me. She was too pale, too thin, and my heart pounded in my throat. I put my hand on her swollen belly, praying for signs of life and the moment my hand touched, a foot found it, but with it came the writhing struggle inside the womb. My children were alive, but they were in as much pain as Naomi.

"It hurts," she whispered, and I pushed her hair away from her face, planting a kiss on her cheek.

"It's going to be all right," I said, even though I didn't believe it, not with our dwindling numbers. Michael and Gabriel went on the offensive, launching a fistfight with Lucifer while we tended to Naomi.

"Can you fix her?" I whispered and then sent a glance in Lucifer's direction in time to see Gabriel fall. He went down hard, the side of his face marred by a red welt where Lucifer had connected. He met my gaze for a moment and then returned to the fight.

Steve bent down and delivered a kiss to Naomi's forehead and light danced over her form, rejuvenating her body, filling her hollow cheeks with a healthy glow. She blinked at him and then her eyes rolled back and she went limp.

"What did you do?" I asked, alarmed by her slip into unconsciousness.

"She'll be fine," Raven said, "But we need to get her out of here," she added, watching the movement of the three archangels. "The path isn't blocked anymore," she said, pointing.

I didn't hesitate. I picked Naomi up and headed for the open escape, and the group followed me. I ran as fast as possible with her limp form in my arms, praying I wouldn't slip. When I reached the back door, I used the power growling inside me to open the locks to the house and burst inside, heading toward the nearest soft surface. The couch sat on the sidewall in the family room with a view of the front yard and lake beyond. I laid Naomi on the soft cushions and pushed her hair away from her face.

"Come on, baby," I whispered, pressing my lips to hers. She didn't respond, and I turned, looking at the crowd behind me.

Raven stepped forward, her gaze averted, but she forced eye contact. "She'll be okay; her life force is still strong." She touched my cheek. "Your babies shine just like you."

I dropped my head to my chest, my relief choking me for a moment before I inhaled and stood, shaking off the momentary lapse. The dull ache in my arms reminded me of my human frailty and I scanned the beautiful view, wondering who would win the battle in the blood-filled clearing.

My answer came a few minutes later, when Lucifer stalked onto the property. The severed heads of my father and uncle dangled from each of his hands and he held them up for me to see. His roar of triumph painted my skin with a burn I hadn't felt since I watched Athena die.

I wanted vengeance, and the power inside me screamed for justice.

"Shit," Ty said from behind me and I turned, staring down the only other angel standing.

I pointed to Naomi. "Keep her safe. That's all I ask," I said, moving my gaze across the faces in the room, then I turned and crossed to the door.

"What do you think you're doing?" Steve asked.

I paused with my hand on the doorknob, asking myself the same question. I glanced out the window and then met Steve's stare dead on.

"Ending this," I said and stepped outside, letting the fury of twenty-five hundred years take over.

Trinity Rising
Chapter Twenty-four
Damian

I STALKED TOWARD LUCIFER, getting my mind in fight mode. A shadow moved into step with me and I glanced at my companion.

"I thought I told you to keep Naomi safe."

"CJ and Steve will see to that," Ty said and met my gaze. "They're making the house safe right now," he added, which meant he wouldn't be able to get back in, and neither would Lucifer if he was the last one standing.

I focused on my nemesis, and he dropped the heads on the ground so they faced me. I ground my teeth together at the manner in which he wiped his hands together, like they were nothing more than dirt and grime. He grinned at me, knowing just how angry I was.

"Coming to exact revenge for your family?" he asked, moving his gaze from me to Ty and back. The question was fitting for both of us, and we stopped less than five paces away.

"Vengeance is mine," I whispered, feeling more like a god than a human at the moment. "And you shall behold the full fury of the heavens."

He laughed, leaning back and cackling to the sky. Ty and I traded a glance and then the angel by my side launched his attack, leaving me standing in a place like a shocked little kid. I blinked as Lucifer went flying on his ass. Ty shook his right hand and then curled it up again as Lucifer got to his feet, his smirk long gone and replaced with wariness.

"I've only felt that kind of power from Michael," he said, narrowing his eyes and studying the angelic form of Ty Ryan. "Gabriel wasn't strong enough to wage any sort of decent fight," he added, stepping away from the discarded heads.

Ty grinned. "The world has never seen anything like me," he said, his voice a feral growl that promised all the pain hell could deliver. "And neither has heaven."

Lucifer waved his hand, and I landed on my ass from the invisible sucker punch. The cold snow seeped into my bloodstained jeans and I climbed to my feet, circling away from Lucifer, letting Ty take the lead in this fight, even though he didn't have the same mental power Lucifer had.

Ty's smile faded when he was shoved a step backwards, but he didn't stumble, he only leveled that glare.

"What are you?" Lucifer asked, unnerved by his inability to budge his primary foe.

"I'm your worst fucking nightmare," Ty said, pulling memory after memory of the same line delivered for the past two decades.

The two angels charged, slamming into each other and creating an explosion that knocked me back twenty feet. Dazed, I pushed into a sitting position, shaking the cobwebs from my head and focused on the flurry of snow before me. The only identifier I could see in the blur was black wings. Ty's blended in with the snow tornado they created.

Blows sounded like thunder, shaking the landscape; and I chanced a glance at the picture window behind me. Steve and Tom had a hold on CJ, his mouth crying out, but the glass prevented me from hearing his wail. I turned back in time to witness the fountain of crimson coming from a headless body kneeling on the ground; blood cascaded down, staining the pristine white wings.

A head rolled on the snow, landing at my feet, and I scrambled into a standing position. The sense of loss coming from the house clouded my vision. My heart ached with sorrow, and I raised my gaze.

Lucifer stepped out of the snow cloud, and I reveled in a moment of satisfaction. Ty had done some damage, but none of it was catastrophic. Lucifer limped forward on a bloodied leg. One of his wrists was twisted enough to elicit a wince from me and his right eye was swollen shut. Even with his injuries, he was a dangerous adversary. I exhaled, stepping into a defensive posture. I would not charge into this blinded by fury. That would only result in the same outcome as Ty, and my father, and Michael.

I was rather fond of having my head attached to my body and I had a family inside to defend, so I proceeded with caution, letting the power coil up inside me, looking for the right moment to strike.

I ignored the belligerent curses coming from CJ; the cautions coming from Steve, and the cries of pain coming from Naomi. I ignored everything but the bastard in front of me.

"I got this," I whispered, and the din in my head lowered.

Lucifer raised an eyebrow, waving me in with the fingers on his good hand. I took a tentative step forward with my heart in my throat and the metallic taste of fear lacing my tongue. New cries filled my mind, and I paused, looking at the snow to my side before bringing my gaze back to Lucifer.

"I'm so looking forward to feeding on a trinity heart, no matter how tainted," he said and looked at my chest. "Especially one containing the grace of two angels."

I let a small laugh escape; he didn't know I was now a father. He didn't know just what kind of strength was building in my bones, and I sidestepped, bringing him away from the house. Away from the heads lying in the snow and towards the pretty little gazebo on the edge of the lake.

The full moon sat high overhead, settling a blue hue over the snow covered world. I glimpsed CJ standing in the window, his glare as deadly as the power coiled in my belly. He met my gaze and the order to make the devil pay rocked my form, but CJ didn't have control over me, just like Steve couldn't get me to relinquish the gun, and my gaze dropped to Lucifer.

Despite their lack of control over my actions, I wholeheartedly agreed with CJ's order.

Lucifer would pay, but I needed information. I needed to know how to fulfill the statement Michael made at the hospital. All I needed now was Lucifer's grace.

"Just out of curiosity, what the hell did Michael mean when he said now all I needed was your grace?" I asked as Lucifer advanced.

He smiled, stalking me like a deadly black panther. "You would become a trinity."

"I thought I already was?" I asked, stalling, stepping further from the house.

"By vampire blood, not by angel grace." He took a step in my direction and I countered, backing up into the half wall of the gazebo.

I had run out of space, and Lucifer knew it. He lunged, pinning me against the post with his injured arm. His glare filling me with dread and the ripping pain that gripped my chest pulled a yelp from my lips. I looked down around the arm, pinning me in place at the fingernails piercing my skin.

My jujitsu maneuvers didn't work, it only proved to further increase the penetration. My base instincts took over and I let out a growl, sinking my teeth into his arm. They broke through the flesh and he howled, pulling away from me. I covered my heart with my left hand and shot my right out in the same dagger like formation as his hand had been.

My fingers sank into flesh and I pushed with both my inertia and my mind, crushing the ribs that stood in my way. I met Lucifer's shocked gaze and smiled as my hand wrapped around his heart. His grace.

He stumbled back, and I yanked with everything I had.

Lucifer landed on his ass with a gaping hole in his chest, but he was still lucid. His wide eyes landing on the pulsing muscle in my hand.

Hot blood ran down my wrist and the thing continued to pulse in my grasp. When I looked beyond the still beating heart and met Lucifer's gaze, I knew I only had a minute to react. He was already climbing to his feet, his features transitioning into fury. If I did the wrong thing, I'd be the one lying dead in the snow.

My stomach rolled at the thought of what I had to do, but I inhaled and brought the heart to my lips.

"No!" he yelled and lunged, but I had already sunk my teeth into the slimy muscle.

Trinity Rising
Chapter Twenty-five
Damian

BLOOD BURNED MY TONGUE, sliding down my throat, and I shoved the rest of his heart in my mouth before he could reach me. His face transitioned from fury to shock to pain with each chew. I struggled not to spit it out, knowing I had to eat the whole thing in order to destroy him.

My throat spasmed, and I stepped up onto the gazebo, forcing breaths through my nose as the vile heart broke down between my teeth. Lucifer crawled forward, and I suppressed my gag reflex, swallowing what chunks were left.

My esophagus clenched, and I fell to my knees, folding over at the pain that bloomed in my core. I grabbed a fistful of snow and shoved it in my mouth to calm the burn.

Lucifer grabbed my wrist, and I yanked away from him, falling back onto my butt.

The power encompassed every fiber, and I bellowed, pushing myself to the opposite wall with my feet. The wounds on my chest formed a patchwork-healing pattern and, after a blink, my skin flushed clear. The wounds disappeared and the power inside me flashed beyond comprehension.

Bitter cold sucked into my lungs as I huffed through the pain gripping me. This was far more painful than the shadow virus had been. It felt like two masses of air ramming into each other, creating an internal tornado. White and dark, fighting for dominance as they melded together into one and CJ's power braided through it like a golden lasso, tying it together and bonding it to every cell in my body.

Lucifer chuckled, his gaze still animated and locked on me. I pushed myself into a standing position and he dragged himself up as well.

Another cry filtered through me, and I looked at the window. My second child. The storm settled like rain and I snapped my gaze back to Lucifer and the gaping hole in his chest.

"So that's how you steal grace," I said and stepped forward, slamming my fist into his face. Bones crunched, and this time, I knew they were his. He flew onto his back on the snow and then turned onto his hands and knees, crawling away.

I stared at the withered wings, feeling a level of triumph I had never known. I always assumed I would die at his hands and a just fury wrapped around my heart. I sent the first blast of power at him, crushing him into the ground.

"Go to hell," I whispered, and the power leaped out, striking with the full force of a flamethrower at point-blank range. Nothing was left but a blackened patch and I stared at it.

Freedom.

The word had a new meaning, and I looked up, crossing the bloody snow to the house that held my future.

A future filled with hope.

Trinity Rising
Chapter Twenty-six
Naomi

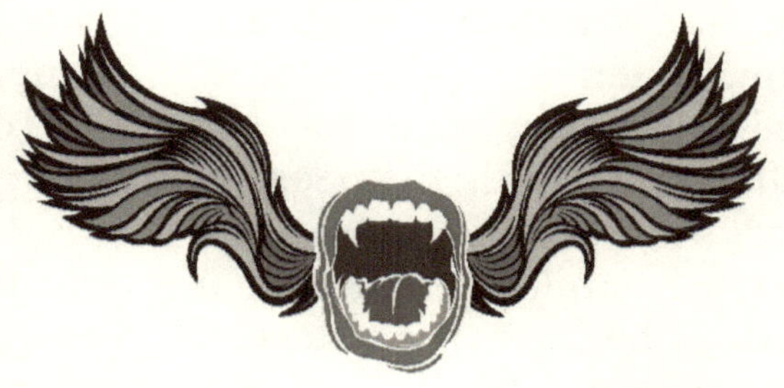

"WHERE IS HE?" I screamed as another contraction crushed my abdomen.

"He's coming," CJ said, and crossed to the door.

A blinding fear filled me, and I didn't understand why CJ would let Lucifer inside. When Damian stepped in the door with blood dripping from his lips, I gasped and the next contraction gripped my stomach. I cried out, grabbing the sides of the couch as Raven wiped my forehead with a damp cloth.

As quickly as it started, it faded, and I breathed a few deep breaths to prepare for the next one, bringing my gaze back to Damian.

He wiped his sleeve across his face, grimacing at the maroon swath it left on the coat. He peeled the fabric off, dropping it on the floor.

"He won't be bothering any of us, ever again," he said, and I blinked, unable to comprehend his words.

Damian's gaze jumped to Tom, and then the baby wrapped in a towel in his arms. It jumped to Steve and the same type bundle wrapped in his arms. When his gaze returned to me, it was filled with wonder and he moved across the floor, dropping to his knees next to me, and pulled my hand to his chest.

His warm smile settled over me, and the next contraction began in earnest. It was like this child waited until her father was at my side. My face scrunched into a mask of pain and I saw the worry in his eyes.

"It's okay," I squeaked out and relief flooded his features.

"Push," Jennifer said, looking down between my legs with the same excitement she had with the first two boys. Raven helped me curl forward; holding her hands on my shoulder blades like Jennifer told her to do.

Damian stared at me, awe painting his features.

"Watch for the baby," I said, each word a pant, and he seemed to snap out of his trance, shifting so he could see what was making Jennifer grin like a madwoman.

"Oh my god," Damian said, his face flushing with anticipation. "I can see the baby's head," he added with a smile. "Keep pushing, sweetheart," he added, with a new level of exhilaration sparkling in his eyes.

The pressure gripped me and I pushed with the last ounce of energy I had and suddenly it released. Jennifer wrapped the third child and smiled.

"You have a girl," she said, and my eyes filled with tears as she handed the third bundle to me. I leaned against Raven and showed her the final perfect child. My little angel looked at me and cooed before her eyes roamed to her father.

"Glad you could make it," I said breathlessly, meeting Damian's glossy gaze.

"You've got two boys and a girl," Jennifer said, glancing at Damian as she swiped up the afterbirth. "And you owe me a new couch," she added with a smile.

"Do you have names picked out?" Steve asked as he looked at his watch and scribbled down the time, along with the date on the paper he had recorded the other births on.

I met Damian's gaze and nodded. "You pick," I said, trusting him to pick the perfect names. I was too exhausted to think and in such awe of the miracles bestowed on us.

"Gabriel Alexander for my first-born boy," he said, and I smiled, feeling the lump form at the homage to the two fallen angels. Damian traded a glance with CJ and got a nod in response. Alexander was his father's middle name, and I knew he had caught the significance.

"Michael for the second." I said. I needed to honor the man who saved Damian from death more than once.

"Michael Christopher," Damian replied, completing the homage to those who saved us from Lucifer today, although I could tell CJ wasn't as comfortable with the honor.

"Hey, I wouldn't have been able to do what I did without that little bit of magic I stole from you," Damian smiled and CJ gave a silent nod, looking down at the baby in his arms.

"I guess that's as good a name as any," he sighed.

"What about her?" I asked and pressed my lips to the baby's forehead.

"Grace," he said before I could formulate a name.

I glanced at Damian as Tommy handed Gabriel to him. The way he looked holding my child made me bit my lip, blinking the tears away, and I glanced back at the baby in my arms.

"Grace?" I asked, and the baby cooed. I smiled at her and tried the name once more time. "Hi, sweet baby, Grace."

Trinity Rising
Epilogue
Damian

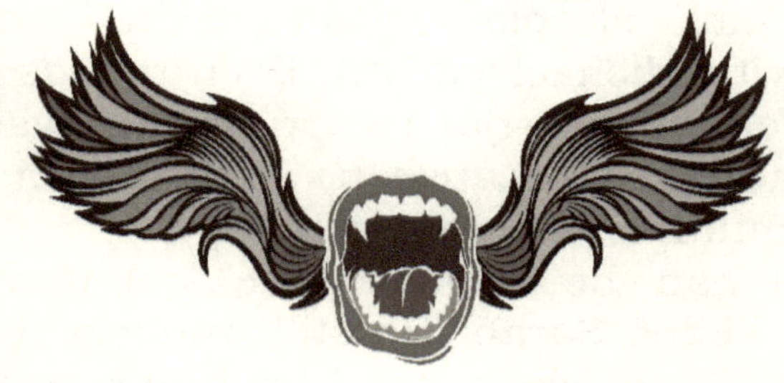

THE KIDS RAN DOWN the beach. Their little legs pumping and their laughter floating on the breeze. I ran after them, pretending to be a big, bad sand monster, catching each one in my arms and rolling onto my back on the sand. Gracie jumped on my chest and her little fingers found the ticklish spots on my neck as Gabe and Michael yelled for help.

I yielded, letting them go and sitting up. All three children gave me fierce hugs, and I looked beyond my five-year-olds at my wife and friends watching in amusement.

The children ran back to the group, and I sighed, feeling the blessings this life had delivered. I stood, swiping the fine grains of sand from my hands, and crossed the distance, settling into the chair next to Naomi and picking up my beer.

Five years had changed all our lives. I still held the power of the trinity as well as the magic CJ had given me. The months following Lucifer's demise had been tough on all of us. For Naomi and me, it was more trying to juggle three infants and sleepless nights than coming to terms with Michael's death. Even the loss of my father felt surreal, but I suppose that was more easily accepted because he hadn't been in my life for multiple millenniums.

Steve had the toughest time dealing with the guilt of killing Sarah. He still wonders if he did the right thing, even when I tell him it was better than the alternative. When he came back from taking us to the hospital, he said the entire place was clear. No blood, no bodies, nothing except the swath of burned ground where I torched Lucifer. As I understand it, Sarah's disappearance from the house in York is still an open case.

Losing Ty hasn't helped him bounce back either. He took it far worse than either CJ or Tom. Regardless of how much he bitched about being saddled with Ty as his guardian angel, the man had become his confidant and best friend.

CJ and Tom adjusted, but then again, they had other things pulling their attention away from their grief.

I sighed, focusing on my daughter. Grace was special in a way that none of us could pinpoint and my boys were just that; wildly active five-year-old identical twins.

Grace wasn't a third identical twin. She hadn't shared the same sac, only the same womb, and the boys adored her. They were fiercely protective of her, just like the rest of us, and I like to think they know she has an extraordinarily rare gene. I like to think they know she's a trinity.

My gaze landed on the birthmark on her right shoulder blade. Doctors had given us shit for years on that, but it was natural and not a tattoo, as they wrongly assumed. As she got older, the details seemed to get crisper, the coloring bolder. When we had checked in at Brooksfield Hospital after the births, they accused us of drawing on our baby girl. That was the first time we saw the etched details of the white-winged tiger mark.

From that day forward, whenever we have blood work done, they always tell us it's been tainted with feline DNA. I just wonder when that tiger is going to come out. I'm hoping it won't make an appearance, but I know that's just wishful thinking.

I stared at the sun-drenched ocean. The light dancing on the waves captured my attention, and I wondered how I got to this wonderful station in life and why I was so lucky.

Naomi's hand covered mine, and I smiled, moving my attention away from the waves.

Some other things have changed for the better, too, and I glanced at two of my closest friends. One has known me since she was born, and I couldn't have picked a better man for her.

Valerie smiled at me like she knew what I was thinking. She ran her hand down CJ's arm and laced her fingers with his.

He turned toward her, returning her grin before his gaze dropped to her oversized belly.

CJ leaned forward, planting a kiss on the swollen skin under her beach dress.

"How you feeling?" he asked.

"Good, considering I'm overdue," she said. "I swear this boy just doesn't want to come out."

Tom and Raven chuckled, turning toward the squealing laugh of their three-year-old daughter. Hannah approached, her tiny hands grasping one of Steve's and Jennifer's. She planted her feet and then jumped, letting Steve and Jennifer swing her forward. Her giggle tickled all of us and we exchanged glances before returning our gaze to the wild redhead. She broke free and ran to our three kids, sliding to a stop and dropping into the sand next to them.

Steve and Jennifer approached, dropping into the vacant seats nearest the kids.

"She's a handful," Steve smiled.

Tom returned his smile, nodding and signing a simple, "Yes."

"Have you settled on a name yet?" Naomi asked, her eyes locked on our children building a sand castle a few feet away.

"Ty," Valerie said, pulling our gazes to her. "Ty Alexander Ryan."

I smiled, scanning the horizon, wondering if Ty was finally at peace in heaven.

Grace stood and crossed to me, taking my hand and meeting my gaze.

"He is, Daddy," she said, patting my hand, leaving tiny traces of sand with each pat.

A chill drifted over all of us and I traded a glance with CJ. He could read me better than anyone here. And he raised his beer in response. Grace seemed to have a line straight to heaven, one that even a trinity of angelic grace didn't have. I gave her a soft smile, staring into those dazzling big blue eyes, and ran my finger down her nose, tapping the end of it lightly.

"Thank you, Grace," I said and wondered just where her celestial knowledge ended. Her level of comprehension never ceased to amaze me, and her insight was always frighteningly accurate, even at five.

"You're welcome, Daddy." She turned, skipping back to the sandcastle.

I knew someday I'd have to worry about Grace, but today wasn't that day.

The End

Continue THE NIGHT HAWK series with
Lilith: A Nighthawk Prequel.

About J.E. Taylor

J.E. Taylor is a USA Today bestselling author, a publisher, an editor, a manuscript formatter, a mother, a wife, a business analyst, and a Supernatural fangirl. Not necessarily in that order. She first sat down to seriously write in February of 2007 after her daughter asked:

"Mom, if you could do anything, what would you do?"
From that moment on, she hasn't looked back.

Besides being co-owner of Novel Concept Publishing, Ms. Taylor also moonlights as a Senior Editor of Allegory, an online venue for Science Fiction, Fantasy and Horror. J.E. Taylor is also one of the co-hosts of the popular podcast <u>Spilling Ink</u>.

She lives in New Hampshire with her husband and two children and during the summer months enjoys her weekends on the shore in southern Maine.

Visit her at <u>www.jetaylor75.com</u> and sign up for her newsletter for early previews of her upcoming books, release announcements, and special opportunities for free swag!